Y0-EKT-526

Savannah's Garden

Susan Cochran

Savannah's Garden

This is a work of fiction. Names, characters, places, and
incidents are products of the author's imagination or are
used fictitiously. Any resemblance to actual events,
locales, organizations, or persons, living or dead, is
entirely coincidental.

No part of this book may be used or reproduced in any
manner whatsoever without written permission except in
the case of brief quotations embodied in critical articles
and reviews.

Without in any way limiting the author's (and publisher's) exclusive
rights under copyright, any use of this publication to "train"
generative artificial intelligence (AI) technologies to generate text is
expressly prohibited. The author reserves all rights to license uses of
this work for generative AI training and development of machine
learning language models.

Copyright © 2025 Susan Cochran

All rights reserved.

ISBN:
ISBN-13: 978-1-967706-01-3

For my writing community friends.
You all are such an inspiration.

1

Parents.

Celine closed her eyes and held the phone to her ear as her mother rattled on.

"Celine, I'm calling about your trip home for Christmas. Should I be expecting only you and Savannah? Or will you be bringing someone with you?"

"Mother, it's only the two of us."

"I hope you haven't been staying at home hiding. Are you dating?"

"Mother, please. I'm not ready to date."

"Celine, you work at a hospital. I'm sure there are lots of single doctors. Put yourself out there. It's the only way you're going to meet someone."

Celine shook her head. "It's too soon."

"Sweetheart, it's been three years already," Marie reminded her. "You don't want to grow old alone. Dex wouldn't want that."

"It's taken me this long to get used to Dex never coming home. I have no desire to go through bad dates and rejection."

"Who wouldn't love you? You're sweet, caring, and a wonderful mother. I'm sure there are loads of single men in

San Francisco just waiting for you."

"Mother…"

"Your mother is here to give you a gentle nudge. It wouldn't hurt to go out on a few dates. If you don't take a risk, you'll never know."

Several of her co-workers and friends had been urging Celine to do just that. Knowing she'd never find another man who would measure up to Dex, she hadn't been interested in dating. Her husband was one of a kind. She'd never meet a man even close to how special he was. Definitely wouldn't if she kept to herself as she had been.

"Don't get too comfortable by yourself. You may want more children someday. Don't wait until you're too old to have them."

"I appreciate the advice, but I have to get Savannah ready for school. See you soon, Mom."

"Give my granddaughter a hug from me. And have her Facetime me when she gets home from school."

"I will." Celine blew out a breath and hung up the phone.

Why won't she ever quit?

Maybe because she's right.

Celine's chest suddenly felt tight. She wasn't afraid of being alone; she had her daughter. But Savannah wouldn't be home with her forever. She'd go on to college and start a career someday. Did Celine want to go through life without someone to share it with? Deep down, she didn't want to be alone. To stop her mother from nagging, she'd consider giving dating a try.

With her dark hair tousled from sleep, six-year-old Savannah stood in the doorway of her mother's bedroom holding a pink elephant, her favorite stuffed animal. "I don't want to go to school today."

Celine turned toward her daughter as she finished dressing. "Today will be a fun day. Miss Callahan has planned a field trip to the firehouse down the street from your school. And I get to chaperone the outing."

"Jana's dad is going, too. And Stacy's dad is a chaperone. You're going to be the only mom."

Celine kneeled down in front of her daughter. "I've never been to a firehouse, so I'm looking forward to seeing it. I wonder if they have a pole to slide down like they do on television shows?"

Savannah wiped her sleepy eyes. "I wish Daddy was here to go with me." Tears trickled down her cheeks.

"I know you do, sweetie. I wish he was here, too." She pulled Savannah into her arms, giving her a warm, loving hug. "Daddy is always with you, here inside your heart." Celine gently placed her hand over Savannah's heart and pressed a kiss on her forehead.

A sudden pain cut through her insides. Celine missed her husband as much as Savannah did.

"Do you think Daddy can see me from up in heaven?"

Her sad eyes caught at Celine's heart. "I know he can. He's your guardian angel, always watching over you."

She nodded, seeming to accept Celine's answer without another thought as she turned to return to her bedroom.

"But now, we need to get moving so we won't be late. Get dressed in the clothes we picked out last night, and eat your breakfast I put on the kitchen table. It's almost time to leave."

Celine rushed to get Savannah to school on time. This seemed to be her life. Rushing here, rushing there. Working, grocery shopping, cooking, and cleaning the house left her exhausted most of the time. The struggling life of a single mother. She was doing her best. It never got easier, and she knew this crazy stage wouldn't last forever, so she'd continue to work hard and make the best life for her daughter.

Savannah had always been an easygoing child. Her sweet little girl was facing her grief head on and Celine wanted to do all she could to help her daughter move forward. Although she thought it would have already happened, Celine knew this day would come. Grief hits everyone differently. Celine had already hit her lowest point since Dex died. It looked as though today would be Savannah's day. She whispered a little prayer and took in a deep breath. She could handle this.

They'd attended therapy, and it had helped. Every Sunday after church, they visit the cemetery to talk to Dex and place flowers on his grave. Savannah looked forward to those days. Keeping to a routine seemed the best way to move back into a normal life. And today, Savannah would go to school as she would any other day.

They walked the few blocks to school. The street was noisy, filled with children in groups, laughing and talking, making their way to one of three different schools in the neighborhood. A charming area of the city with rows of two-story homes, many with multi-generation families, and neatly kept yards filled with colorful flowers.

Celine watched as a police car drove past, and an unwanted flash of memory filled her mind. The sight of any police car gave her chills and instantly triggered memories of the day of the incident at the shopping mall where her husband died.

She longed for the days before the shooting. Before she'd became a widow. A label she never wanted and wouldn't wish any woman to experience.

She could never forget the morning she kissed her husband goodbye before he left for work. Could never forget the look of love in his eyes or the warmth of his embrace.

"Call the sitter. Tonight, I'm taking my wife out. Just you and me. A nice dinner and a bottle of wine," Dex had told her. He'd

brushed a kiss on her lips before leaving. The last moment they'd ever have.

Celine swallowed past the lump in her throat and brushed aside the memory. Now wasn't the time to think about him. If she did, she'd only cry.

They entered the schoolyard just as the bell rang. Celine saw Bridget Callahan, Savannah's teacher, lining up the children to go inside the school. Bridget was one of the reasons Celine loved the school. She had been Savannah's kindergarten teacher, then Bridget switched to teach first graders. Savannah was fortunate to get Bridget again as her teacher. Over the past year, Celine and Bridget had become good friends.

Bridget cared about the students, and it showed with her interactions with the children. The popular teacher was smart and gorgeous and incredibly sweet. The kids loved her.

And so did the kids' dads. She had the silky chocolate-colored hair and curvy body they all lusted over.

Celine placed a gentle hand on her daughter's shoulder. "We're going to have fun on your field trip."

After calling roll, the class walked in a single file to the neighborhood firehouse. Jack, one of the firefighters, gave them a tour of the firehouse, showing the kids where they sleep, the day room where they relax between calls, and the enormous kitchen where they eat.

"Do you have to cook?" one little boy asked the firefighter giving the tour.

"Only if we want to eat. Trust me, this job will make you hungry."

After a lesson on fire safety, including instructions on stop, drop, and roll, the group proceeded to the apparatus floor, where they kept the fire engines and trucks. Jack gave each child a *chief's badge* sticker to put on their shirt and a plastic firefighter helmet to wear. The children loved climbing into the fire trucks to pretend they were on their way to an emergency. They were thrilled.

Seeing the smile on Savannah's face helped lift the heaviness in Celine's heart. For now, she seemed to be doing okay.

As the class stood outside near the fire trucks and were getting ready to leave, a tall, well-built man wearing a dark-blue fire department uniform walked in. He stopped short when he saw the group of children and parents. He looked directly toward Bridget, who looked none too happy.

"Sorry I'm late. I'll take it from here," he said to the firefighter giving the tour.

"We've just finished."

"This is my brother, Anthony," Bridget said as an introduction. "The same brother who promised to give the class a tour of the firehouse, but he failed to show."

"Sorry about that. Got my days mixed up. I was teaching a class for the new recruits," Anthony said.

"It's fine. Jack took care of us and gave the class a great tour," Bridget said, glancing at Jack and sent a sweet smile his way.

"It's not fine. I apologize. Can I make it up to you?" Anthony said to Bridget. "Dinner?"

"Call me later. Just warning you, it's going to cost you."

"No doubt."

"I'll talk to you soon," Bridget said as she led her class out the door and back toward the school.

2

On their way home after school, Celine stopped at the neighborhood bakery, which had holiday wreaths displayed in every window. There was a steady stream of people going in and out of the shop, chatting and laughing.

Celine opened the door and the aroma of freshly baked goodies engulfed her. Inside, the long display case was full of delectable pastries, cookies, and cupcakes. They picked up two apple fritters for the following morning.

"How about a special Christmas cookie for you?" the saleslady asked, looking at Savannah.

"Mommy, can I?" she asked her mother with pleading eyes.

"Only if you promise to eat all your vegetables tonight."

Savannah smiled. "I promise."

After dinner that night, Celine called out to Savannah to come out of her bedroom to talk.

Her little round face beamed as she walked into the living room carrying her special memory box.

"What do you have there?" Celine asked.

"Daddy's special box."

Celine's heart lurched to her throat.

Dex's mother, Linda, had given it to Savannah soon after

Dex died. It had been his own treasure chest when he was a boy. A special box that held all his most prized possessions, including a favorite stuffed animal, a little blue elephant that had been his when he was a child.

Savannah treasured it. She added to the box a few special trinkets her father had given her and pictures of them together. Whenever Savannah wanted to feel close to her father, she would get the treasured box from her closet and sit down on her bed and open it.

But today, Savannah held it for the longest time without opening it. A sadness seemed to move through her. This year would be another Christmas that Dex wouldn't be here with them. Celine was sure it was affecting her. The thought of Savannah missing out on spending the holidays with her father often left her heavyhearted.

"Can I look at it with you?"

Savannah climbed up on the sofa and set it between them. She opened the box and took out a Matchbox car that had belonged to her father when he was a child. "Grandma told me Daddy loved this when he was little. When I'm sad, I like looking through this box. It makes me happy."

"What else helps you push aside the sadness?"

"My colored rocks."

Celine smiled, thinking about the colored rocks they painted one rainy day.

"I don't play with cars. Do you think Daddy would be mad if I gave it to a boy who likes cars?"

Warmth flowed through Celine's heart. "I think your father would think it a wonderful idea."

Celine often talked of Dex with Savannah. She never wanted her to forget her father. He had loved Savannah more than anything. Watching her daughter grow up without him tore at her heart.

Celine and Dex had built a life in San Francisco. He loved

his career at the San Francisco Police Department, and they had bought their first home here. With their daughter, they had a good life. Savannah was six now, and the only reason Celine kept it together. She put Savannah before everything else in her life.

She observed Savannah holding a picture of herself with her father. Celine smiled at the memory of Dex and at how he always took photos of Savannah. Dex was a good, decent man. He loved being a father. It gave Celine some solace that Savannah had so many photos of herself with him. She only wished Savannah had more time with Dex. An ache filled her heart. An ache shared with her daughter.

Looking down at Savannah going through Dex's things, it hurt to believe that other than her memories, this might be all she had left of Dex. She'd never hold him again, never hear his voice. And he'd never see Savannah grow up into a young woman. Dex would never meet their little girl's first boyfriend, or watch her high school graduation, never walk her down the aisle when she married.

Oh, Dex, why did they have to take you from us?

Celine pulled her daughter against her and hugged her tight. She wanted Savannah to never forget her father or how much he loved her. Just as Celine would never forget him or the love they shared. The only man she ever loved. She couldn't imagine loving another man as much as she loved Dex. So much had changed without him in their lives. It was just so hard to let go of him and get on with her life.

Would she always feel this way?

Celine didn't have time to date. Oh, there were single doctors at the hospital who had asked her out over the last few years. But her daughter came first, and with all her activities, it left Celine little time to think of her own social life. Or have the energy for one if she had one. At times she wanted to close off the world, hide, and not be around anyone. Didn't want to interact with friends or colleagues. Her therapist diagnosed her with mild depression. Her mother called it grieving. They both said that with time, it would get better. They were right. It had eased some.

On the bookshelf, she glimpsed the family portrait they had taken right before that fateful day. Their last day together as a family.

The memories were still so fresh. Raw. Heartbreaking.

Memories of good times were still there, but she struggled at times to push the bad ones to the back of her mind. Her husband's funeral—the miles-long procession of cars passed before her. It had been three years since Dex had died in the line of duty, but it still seemed like yesterday.

Celine didn't want to be reminded of the raw pain, but she had to face it head on if she wanted to help Savannah with her own sorrow. It was hard, but she pushed forth for her daughter's sake. She was her priority. The only one who mattered.

A mixture of compassion and heartache moved through Celine as she looked at her daughter, who seemed to do so well most days. Then, at times, the sadness barreled through her with a vengeance. She worried about the lasting impact their loss would have on Savannah, but resigned herself that Savannah would move forward at her own pace as she processed the changes to their lives. They were both strong and resilient, and with that thought, Celine felt she would pull through.

Savannah's voice brought her out of her thoughts. "Mommy, what if...we made a Christmas garden in front of our house? I can put some of my favorite things in it and some of my little toys I don't play with. Kids walking to school will see it as they pass our house. If some kids are feeling sad, like me, I think it may help to make them happy."

"Giving hope and joy to other children going through a

hard time as you are is a wonderful idea."

Savannah jumped off the sofa and stood at the big picture window overlooking their front yard. "Ryan's big brother is in the Army and won't be home for Christmas, and he's sad. Katie's grandparents are on a trip and she won't see them until they come home."

Celine wasn't feeling particularly festive this year. The thought of Christmas without Dex put a damper on her holiday spirit, but for her daughter, she would push through her own issues and make it special for Savannah.

Five minutes later, Savannah came back from her bedroom and handed her mother a colorful bracelet she made and a sparkly green dice she no longer played with. "Someone else may like this more than me. Do you think Santa Claus would take these and the little car and give it to someone who would play with it?"

"I'm sure he would find someone. Or we could leave the garden in place for other children to enjoy. After Christmas, you can donate the toys you don't want to keep to the homeless shelter. I'm sure another child would love to have any of your special gifts you want to share with them."

"That's what I want to do, Mommy."

3

Anthony Callahan often walked home from the firehouse after his shift ended. A few blocks through the business district, to the residential neighborhood, to his house. Small storefronts displayed strings of Christmas lights, and the city had decorated the street lampposts with garland and silver bells. Anthony turned the corner and noticed a festive garden that someone had set up in a planter box at the base of a tree. It didn't look like anything the city had done. It intrigued him, and upon closer inspection, he realized it was a Christmas garden made by a young child.

There were a few little objects placed in the garden, complete with a small Christmas tree, and a little note about the six-year-old girl who felt lonely. She wanted to spread some holiday cheer.

The note read—

My six-year-old daughter is missing someone special to her. Savannah made this garden to brighten your day in case you are also missing someone this Christmas. Please add to the magic, but don't take anything away. She has left her special treasures for everyone to enjoy. Many of us have hard times during the holidays, but remember to spread cheer and goodwill to everyone. Your heart will feel fuller and brighter. So please enjoy our Christmas garden and have a good day.

Brightly painted rocks and little notes with children's pictures were left there. A bright red Matchbox car, friendship bracelets, and a sparkly green dice held their own place under the Christmas tree.

Anthony generally avoided anything to do with Christmas or the holidays. It brought back too many painful memories of what he once had. What he had lost.

He pushed open the front door of his home and stopped in his tracks. In the entryway, he came face to face with a photo of himself with Lily. His wife. The woman he had been married to for six months. Her life cut short by a drunk driver. The loss still stung. It likely always would. Some days were better than others. Seeing the little holiday garden reminded him of how Lily had loved Christmas. Perhaps he would add to the garden a little something in Lily's honor. She'd like that.

He moved into the kitchen to make a smoothie. Within five minutes, the doorbell rang. He shouldn't have been surprised to see his sister, Bridget, standing in the doorway. Her cheery expression changed quickly into a scowl when she made her way into the living room and scanned the room, absent of a Christmas tree.

"You don't even have a tree up, *grinch*," Bridget admonished him, knowing full well his reasoning.

"You know why I avoid it."

"I understand, but it's been four years. Time to move forward. Shake things up and brighten your place. It may change your outlook on life."

"My outlook is fine."

"Whatever you say, *grumpy bear*."

"I apologize for flaking out on your school tour."

"Don't worry about it. Jack was happy to fill in."

Anthony sent her a grin. "Only because he's dying to take you out, but you keep brushing him off, making excuses."

"He's not my type. Besides, I have other things going on besides hooking up with one of your buddies."

"Such as?"

"This weekend, I'm attending a women's rights march. I hardly think he'd be interested in the same things as I am."

"You never know unless you get to know him. He's a good guy."

Bridget rolled her eyes. "The last *good guy* you fixed me up with believed a woman's place was at home, pregnant, and the most difficult decision of her day should be deciding what to cook her man for dinner. You know me better than to think I'll ever date one of *those* guys again."

Anthony laughed. "So what are you doing here besides busting my balls?"

"We need to talk about Christmas. Dad wants all of us at home this year. He wasn't happy with Rob and Christian going off to Cabo last year. Dad's getting older, so we should all spend the day with him."

"He's not *that* old."

"Regardless, we should all be together for Christmas dinner."

"Count me in. I work on Christmas Eve and get off in the morning. I planned on covering a few hours for one of the guys on Christmas morning so he can open presents with his kids, but I'll be off by noon. That is, if no one calls in sick on Christmas."

"Since you're off today, I'm here to make you put up a tree. No more bah humbug and all that nonsense."

"Okay, *Miss Bossy Pants*, why don't you help me decorate it?"

"Exactly the reason I'm here. Let's get your decorations

out."

They went to the attic and pulled a small artificial tree downstairs. There were two boxes of ornaments Lily had picked out that he'd kept. They settled it all in the living room and began going through the decorations.

As Anthony was looking through one box, he found a red heart lucky charm he won at the county fair one year. He'd given it to Bridget, and when he tested for the fire department, she'd given it back to him for luck. It worked, and he got the job all those years ago.

He couldn't believe he still had it and had no clue how it ended up in the box of ornaments where it didn't belong.

She snatched it out of his hand. "I can't believe you still have this. It always made me smile when I remembered where we got it and how much fun we had that day." She handed it back to him.

Her words held weight, and an idea hit him as he held it in his hand.

On his way to the firehouse for his next shift, Anthony stopped at the tree with the Christmas garden encircling it. He left Savannah, the little girl who made the garden, a note, pretending to be an elf named Teddy who lived in the tree when he wasn't busy at the North Pole. Teddy's assignment from Santa Claus was to keep watch over all the treasures that Savannah had left so nicely.

The note read—

To Savannah and all my new friends,

My name is Teddy. I am an elf from the North Pole. Santa Claus and Mrs. Claus sent me to sprinkle good cheer throughout the area. When Santa saw this beautiful Christmas garden, he asked me to keep watch over it. He thought it was a garden made with love and truly special in his eyes.

Santa gave me a magical lucky charm, but I have no need for it because I am already a lucky elf who lives at the best place ever...the North Pole! After seeing this wonderful garden, it gave me an idea. Maybe you would like it?

I will live here in this tree for a short time and want to give it to you, but first, you need to prove you are worthy. Only the nicest, kindest people may have the lucky charm. So here's what you need to do for me before I can give you this special North Pole edition lucky charm.

Promise to always be kind and show love to those in need.

Say five nice things to people you love.

Do three helpful things for someone in need.

Draw a picture of yourself so I can show Santa and Mrs. Claus.

If these things are done, and you leave me a little note telling me you've completed your tasks, I will leave the lucky charm here on Saturday morning for you to enjoy.

Be sure to share with me if anyone helps you with these tasks. Good luck and love will come to you both.

Love, Teddy

He wasn't sure if she'd find the note or respond, but it was fun to imagine what she'd think if she did.

4

Celine watched her daughter's eyes full of excitement as they went inside the animal shelter. It was Savannah's idea to volunteer at the shelter, believing it would accomplish a helpful thing for someone in need. The cats needed attention and love.

"It's so cold here," Savannah said into her mittens as she held them up to her face to warm her cold nose. "I think the blankets we brought will help keep the kittens warm."

"I know many kittens will be thrilled to have the nice blankets you brought us," Katie, the shelter volunteer, said while taking the donation and setting it aside. "Savannah, your mother told me on the phone that you both would like to volunteer today."

"Yes, I promised Teddy, Santa's elf, that I would do three helpful things for someone in need."

Katie exchanged a look with Celine, who had explained on the phone their challenge, and she smiled back at Savannah. "Our kittens are still young and not up for visitors yet, but I know two older cats who are very excited to meet you. I'll take you to see them."

Katie led the way inside the cat kennel, where there were dozens of adorable cats up for adoption. She settled them in an enclosed visiting room before bringing in two cats who had been at the shelter the longest.

"This one is cute. And she's purring," Savannah said about the cat she held in her lap, stroking the cat's tiny head with her thumb.

"That means you're making her happy. Her name is Tucker. She likes you."

"Tucker is a boy's name," Savannah said, giggling.

"That's because the couple who had her thought she was a boy cat," Katie said.

"Why isn't she still with them?"

"They had to move far away and couldn't take her," Katie told them before leaving the room.

"I like her," Savannah announced, holding the cat against her chest.

Celine noted how her face beamed with joy, her smile wide and genuine. She scooped up the other cat into her arms. He rubbed his face against her before jumping off her lap to the floor and scratching at the door. A definite sign that the cat needed more human interaction. That, or she doesn't like Celine.

"Mommy, look!"

Celine laughed as Tucker crawled onto Savannah's shoulder and settled her long body around Savannah's neck.

Katie peeked her head into the room and picked up the black cat at the door. "How's everything going?"

"Little Blackie has things to do, places to go, and people to see. And that doesn't include us," Celine replied.

"Don't take it personally. He's not a *people cat*." Katie glanced at Savannah and noted the pure joy on her face. "The tabby is another story. She'll sit in your lap all day if you let her. She's our little love bug."

"Mommy, she's so sweet."

"I'll take this unsociable guy back to his comfort zone. Be

back in a few." Katie left and settled the black cat back into its metal cage.

Savannah continued to talk to Tucker as she curled up into her lap and purred. She was in love with her.

After some time had passed, Celine glanced at her watch. "Our time is about up. We have to give her back so someone else can use the petting room."

Savannah hesitated to hand over the tabby to Katie when she returned. The cat meowed, upset at having to leave Savannah's warm and comfortable lap.

They walked through the room lined with dozens of cages housing one, two, or sometimes three cats. Several vocalized their objections of being ignored and meowed loudly.

"Mommy, they look so sad. I wish I could bring them all home."

Celine had thought for months about letting Savannah get a pet. She'd been a great help around the house and proved herself as responsible. As much as a six-year-old could be. Today seemed as good a day as any to fulfill her feline yearnings.

Celine stopped her in front of the tabby's cage. Tucker rubbed against the cage, begging to be petted and loved. The cat looked at Celine with loving eyes and meowed. Savannah looked up at her mother with pleading eyes.

The sweet faces staring back at her swayed Celine. She caved to the pressure. "If you promise to feed and water her, you may adopt the tabby and bring her home. But only her."

"But she'll be so lonely without a friend."

"You're her friend."

"I'm her mommy."

"You can be a friend and a mommy at the same time," Celine said.

Savannah did not look convinced.

"I'm your mommy, right?"

Savannah giggled. "Yes, silly mommy."

Celine returned a smile. "Am I your friend, too?"

"Yes."

"And there you are, proving my point."

Savannah let out a squeal of delight and flung her arms around her mother. "Thank you, Mommy! I promise to take good care of her!"

Celine's heart warmed, delighted to make her daughter so happy.

On the way home, they stopped at a local pet store. Celine purchased cat food, a litter box, a pink sparkly cat bed, and other essentials they would need.

Savannah selected a royal blue collar for the cat, along with several toys and small rubber balls for her to chase. On their way to the register to pay, Celine noticed the all important cat scratcher post and picked one up and put it in her shopping cart.

As they drove home, Celine glanced in the rearview mirror and saw the enormous smile on Savannah's face. She smiled back. Giving Savannah a sense of normalcy by having a pet was the right thing to do.

5

It was nine in the morning when Anthony and his crew finally made it back to the fire station. The fire alarm woke them at four in the morning and they responded to a three-alarm blaze. When they arrived, flames fully engulfed the two-story structure. Fortunately, the residents were away, so no one got hurt.

After the firefighters knocked down the fire and mopped up, Anthony was exhausted by the time he returned to the firehouse. The oncoming shift had a full pot of hot coffee brewed and cooked breakfast for them all. A welcome gesture for the hungry men.

On his way home from the firehouse, Anthony passed the garden. It had been a busy, hectic night, and he hadn't given it a second thought. Then something told him to turn around.

When he saw the note, he was glad he had.

The note read—

Dear Teddy,

I can't believe you left me a note! I called both of my grandmas and grandpas and great-grandma Joan and told them I loved them.

I picked up trash around the neighborhood today.

I set the table and helped my mommy cook dinner.

I promise to be kind and always show love to those in need. Like I did at the animal shelter. Mommy and I volunteered and spent time with the cats. Mommy even let me adopt one! Her name is Tucker, a silly name for a girl. She's so sweet and cuddly and sleeps with me!

I hope you like the picture I made for you. I am so excited about the special lucky charm!

Your friend, Savannah

The note re-energized him and left him in a great mood. He was happy to have given the child a smile.

Anthony drove by the garden on his way to his brother's office. He noticed two children staring at little trinkets someone had left. A broad grin crossed his face, thinking about the little girl who made the garden, wishing he could see her face when she found the lucky charm he promised to leave. He had safely tucked the charm into his pocket, along with a note, but he couldn't let anyone see him when he left it.

He went on to Rob's office for their meeting. The lobby of the building was relatively busy as he made his way to the elevator. Typical for a weekday in a towering skyscraper in the financial district of San Francisco. At least thirty people stood in line at the Starbucks on the ground floor. He imagined their profit margin from this store alone would cover at least a half dozen underperforming locations.

Rob ran Callahan Software, their father's tech company. Although his title as CFO designated him in charge of the financial aspects of the company, Andrew had stepped back considerably and relinquished a large amount of the day-to-day operations to Rob, who would eventually lead the company.

Anthony popped a breath mint before the elevator came to

a stop on the seventeenth floor. Stepping out, he greeted several employees gathered in the lobby. They replied with their own morning greetings, recognizing the company founder's son, and immediately scattered, not wanting to be caught loitering when they should be working, even though Anthony had no official capacity in the business.

"Good morning, Mr. Callahan. You can go right in, Mr. Callahan is expecting you," Alana, Rob's executive assistant, said, flashing a flirtatious smile his way.

The door behind her desk stood propped open. Rob stood when he saw Anthony approaching.

"Come on in, Anthony. Can I get you a coffee? Anything to drink?"

"I'd rather you get to the point of this meeting. If you want to see me and hang out, I'd rather you bring a six-pack of beer on a Sunday and we could watch the 49ers play."

"Have you given any more thought to coming on board at the company? I could really use you here," Rob offered.

Anthony's deep voice rumbled. "You inherited the top position at the company, and I'm happy for you. The job suits you. I'm happy to help you out with some of the charities, but that's as far as my involvement will be."

"Give it some thought before you make a final decision."

"Like I told you before, I've got the best job in the world. I'm a firefighter, happy being out in the community. I've no desire to push paperwork and work in a corporate environment. Even for Dad."

"You're a stubborn cuss, just like Dad."

Anthony had to laugh. "It's the stubborn Irish blood in my veins. Tends to run in the family, wouldn't you agree?"

"I had to ask. But if you change your mind…"

"I won't."

They discussed a new phone app in development that would show any emergency in any city in North America.

Anyone with an iPhone would be able to keep apprised of what goes on in their town. They would be able to see the location of any emergency on a map and listen to the dispatcher and crews on the scene. San Francisco Fire Department would be the first department featured and tested with.

"While you're here, stop by Christian's office," Rob added. "I believe he has the check ready for the donation to your fire department's toy drive. I'm sure it will help in providing the city's underprivileged children a happy holiday."

"It will make a big impact. Thanks."

"Don't thank me. I think we can all agree that children deserve to have a little joy in their lives, regardless of their parent's income."

"Right you are."

After their meeting, Anthony headed home. The street was empty of people near the little garden. He looked around and pulled the note he'd written from his pocket. He placed the note and the small, red charm inside the garden.

Dear Savannah,

You passed the test! This is a very special lucky charm handmade by an elf at the North Pole. As long as you always follow your heart and are a kind person, this charm will give you good luck forever! You deserve it!

The elves at the North Pole love you!

Your friend, Teddy

Anthony enjoyed doing something fun for the child and wished he could see the look on her face when she found it. He also left another note for the little girl's parents with his name and phone number so they could contact him and know he wasn't some creep, leaving notes for their daughter.

The next morning after his run, Anthony stopped by the garden. There was an older woman there admiring it.

"Nice garden, isn't it?" she commented after dropping a few shiny pennies under the tree.

They chatted for a few minutes before she went on her way. He found a note from Savannah written on the same pink stationery as her other notes.

Dear Teddy,

I love the charm! It's beautiful! What is the name of the elf who made it?

My mommy helped me attach the charm to a necklace and now I can wear it always and have good luck forever. Please have a Merry Christmas!

I love you, Savannah.

P.S. My mommy showed me on a map where the North Pole is. You're so far away. I hope you aren't homesick. I know I would be if I were away from my mommy. Have a safe trip once you go back home.

Anthony noticed Savannah didn't mention a father. Was her mother a single mother? What a tough job in these times to raise a child by herself, if that was the case. Then he noticed another note left for *Teddy*.

Dear Teddy,

Thank you so much for living in this special neighborhood tree. You have been a much needed bright spot in our holiday season. The lucky charm is such a sweet gift and not at all lost on us. We hope you are safe and well. We're so glad you visited our garden.

Celine

Celine?

Doesn't Bridget have a friend named Celine? Could this Celine be Bridget's friend?

Nah. Couldn't be.

They left notes for each other over the next few days. He kept the most recent one in his jacket pocket. Whenever he was feeling down, he'd pull out the note and read it. The notes brightened his day, leaving the gloom he had experienced far behind, and left him with the true meaning of the holiday season.

Anthony got to chat with Savannah's mom via text and at one point, she asked to meet for coffee to thank him in person. He suspected what she wanted to do was to make sure he was not a pervert leaving notes for little girls. How could he blame her?

They made a date to have coffee the next day.

6

They planned to meet at a coffee shop a few blocks away from the garden. The shop has notoriously great coffee, often with lines of customers extending out the door. Today it was surprisingly empty.

Celine told him she'd wear a red scarf so he could find her. After she'd gotten her hazelnut latte, she found a table by the window and wouldn't be hard to miss.

The bell over the door of the coffeehouse rang out, and she watched as three customers moved to the counter to order their coffee. She scrutinized each one. Celine had a six-year-old daughter who was her priority. She didn't trust easily where Savannah was concerned, no matter how friendly and pleasant their texts had seemed.

Within minutes, the sound of footsteps moved toward her. Celine's attention turned away from an older couple nearby, laughing and chatting. She noticed a man holding a cup in his hand stop a few feet away and look around. He looked familiar. She watched him, curious if he was the elf. Her skeptical eyes met his.

Then the man, wearing jeans molded to his thighs, and a navy blue T-shirt with the fabric straining to contain his biceps, moved in her direction. She couldn't tear her eyes away from him. His dark hair was messy, slightly damp, as if he just stepped from the shower.

Her eyes softened as recognition hit her.

The firehouse.

"Anthony?" she asked.

"You look familiar. Have we met before?"

"You're Bridget Callahan's brother," she stated, sure of herself. "We met at your firehouse. Well, we didn't actually *meet.* Bridget introduced you to the class. My daughter is in Bridget's class."

A warm, easy smile lit up his face. "The school tour. Now I remember. I hope you haven't been waiting long."

"Only a few minutes."

"We had an early morning fire, and I just got back to the station." Anthony held his hand out. "It's nice to meet you."

When she touched her hand to his, there was a spark. A connection. Quickly recovering from the moment, she studied him, a bit perplexed. "And you're…Teddy?"

"Guilty as charged."

"You hardly look like the elf I envisioned. Knowing you're Bridget's brother and not a crazy person stalking little girls gives me some comfort."

He grinned. "There are too many of those types in the city. You can't be too careful nowadays."

Relief flooded her. At six-feet two, with broad shoulders and a body of solid muscle, Anthony's looks could be intimidating. But as someone who would do such a kind deed for a little girl, she suspected underneath the hulking physique he was a big teddy bear with a heart. An attractive teddy bear with a ruggedly handsome face. A far cry from any of Santa's helpers she had seen before.

Noting her wary expression, Anthony gave her a warm smile. "I walk by the tree on my way to the firehouse for my shift."

"And you stopped. Tell me about why you wrote my daughter the note?"

He let out a sigh and paused a moment. "Holidays haven't been the most joyous for me. When I stopped and read the note, it made me smile. This little girl thought to think of others and hopefully brighten their day. The goodness in her heart made an impression on me. To tell you the truth, she made my day. I thought to do the same for her."

The kind gesture launched her heart into her throat. "It was sweet of you. You also made her day. I don't think she's smiled this much in quite some time. After school, she looks forward to stopping by the garden."

As she sipped her coffee, Celine gathered that Anthony Callahan was a kind man. For someone to go out of his way to do a gesture so sweet for her daughter meant a lot to her.

When Anthony first noticed Celine sitting at the table wearing a white sweater with a red scarf at her throat, he couldn't take his eyes off her. The woman looked so calm and pretty. With his attention turned toward her, the world tilted.

My God, she's beautiful.

A dimple pierced his cheek as the muscle in his jaw moved, causing an instant smile to cross over his face. His feet had propelled him forward without thinking.

His gaze focused on her the entire time they talked, trying not to stare at her eyes, noting how deep blue they were, fringed with thick, dark lashes. But he couldn't help himself, so he did look. She intrigued him. A woman as confident and beautiful as Celine had awakened places inside him he'd forgotten existed.

They chatted about his work as a firefighter at the neighborhood firehouse. The conversation stayed casual as he tried to put her at ease.

"Are you a local?" Celine asked. "Did you grow up in San Francisco?"

"I was born and raised in Pensacola. Dad was a Navy flight officer."

"That sounds exciting."

He half shrugged with a grin. "It had its moments. The drinking age on base was only eighteen. Me and my brothers got to know the bartender at the NCO club fairly well. What about you? A native Californian?"

"Unfortunately, I grew up in snowy Connecticut."

"What is it you do?"

"I'm a pediatric RN."

"A challenging job. You're good with children."

Her face lit up. "I love children."

He was drawn to her. The attraction was strong. He couldn't take his eyes off her pink lips and wondered if they were as soft and supple as they looked. And the rest of her? He imagined under that sweater her skin was even softer. A shiver shook him and he thought to bring his caveman mind down a notch.

A woman as pretty as Celine most likely wasn't unattached. She could be someone's wife or girlfriend. His eyes went to her left hand, holding her cup.

No ring.

He couldn't help himself. "I may be out of line here, but would you like to have dinner sometime?"

She looked surprised at the question. "Like on a date?"

"Yes, a date, you and me."

"I don't date."

He gestured toward her left hand. "I noticed you don't wear a wedding ring. You're not married, are you?"

She shook her head.

"I'm sorry if I overstepped. You must have a boyfriend."

"I'm a widow."

Anthony noted the brief moment of sadness cross her face. "Forgive me. I'm sorry for your loss."

She lowered her eyes with a slight nod of her head.

"Did you lose him recently?" he asked.

"It's been three years."

"It can't be easy to be a single mother."

"It can be hard at times. Luckily, I have an extraordinary, easygoing daughter. We have each other and make it work."

"Your daughter is a kind soul. She must get that from her mother."

She bit down on her lower lip, fighting her emotions. With a deep breath, she explained. "Savannah is six. She was three when her father died. Somehow, she still remembers her last Christmas morning with her father. This year, she's having a rough time. Savannah wanted to make the garden to give hope to anyone else who was experiencing the holiday blues."

"I'm sorry to hear she's having a hard time." Continuing to hold her gaze, he wanted to know more. "May I ask how he died?"

"Her father was a police officer here in the city. There was an active shooter at the mall. Dex died protecting a grandmother and her three granddaughters."

Anthony took in a sharp breath and bowed his head, running his hand over his jaw. "I was there that day on duty. Your husband was a hero."

"Did you know Dex Monroe?"

He snapped his gaze to hers. "He used to stop at the firehouse sometimes to use the head and grab a cup of coffee. Dex was a great guy. I'm sorry, Celine."

She leaned back in her chair, biting back tears. "I was at the park with Savannah, unaware of what was happening at the mall. We were walking back to the house when I noticed the police car parked out front. It's never good news when the police chief comes to your door." She swiped away a fallen tear.

"You must miss him."

"I do, unbearably at times. But I keep moving forward. There's Savannah to think about."

"Your daughter is a special child. Quite thoughtful for being so young."

"Yes, she is. And she keeps me on my toes. Which means I need to get moving before school lets out. I'm happy to have met you. Thank you for spreading a little Christmas cheer for my daughter."

"Bring her by the firehouse sometime. I'll give you both a tour."

"We'd like that, thanks." She stood and headed out the door.

As Anthony followed her out and walked in the opposite direction, he chanced to glance over his shoulder, his gaze trailing after her, telling himself that maybe this Christmas would be a turning point in his life.

7

The idea of having three weeks off from work excited Celine. It had been a busy, challenging day at the hospital with several new admissions. The thought of a child spending time in the hospital during the Christmas holidays broke her heart. Before she left for work, she had made a huge batch of brownies for the kids able to eat solid food and enjoy the sweet treat. It wasn't much, but any little gesture she could do for the children helped ease her heart. Whatever she could do to brighten someone else's holiday helped to lessen her own sadness she suffered through at this time of the year.

The last three years had been difficult for her and Savannah, and Celine promised to make this year one of the best for her daughter.

Celine rushed from work to the school to pick up Savannah. She pulled to the curb outside the school, where Savannah waited with the rest of her classmates and their teacher.

"Goodbye, Miss Callahan," Savannah said with a wave as they left.

The trip home normally took three minutes. Today, traffic had backed up considerably. Several police cars and fire trucks raced through the area to an emergency with their lights flashing and sirens blaring. A traffic cop stood in the middle of the intersection, diverting cars from her street.

"I need to get through. I live on this block," Celine told the officer.

"Not going to happen, ma'am. Fire department has the street blocked off. A house caught fire."

"Oh, my God! Do you know which house it is?" She craned her neck, peering around the policeman and the flurry of activity to see if she could make out which house. All she could see was a thin plume of black smoke curling upward into the sky from halfway down the street.

"It's a two story gray house. They said no one was home and we're trying to figure out how to contact the homeowner."

Icy fear ran up her spine. She had the only gray house on the block. "It's my house!"

The cop scanned the street. "Go park over there." He directed Celine to a space on the street.

With parking nearly nonexistent in the city, somehow Celine maneuvered her vehicle into the tiny space between two cars. Her heart fell as she grabbed Savannah's hand and rushed to get as close as she could get to see how bad the fire was. Suddenly, the air felt as though it had been sucked from her body. They stood watching smoke pour out of the kitchen windows and flames lick at the sills in her beloved home she had lived in for the last eight years. The shrill sound of smoke alarms rang out. Celine stood by, wringing her hands. She worried about Tucker. Their cat would normally be asleep on top of Savannah's bed during the day. Hopefully, she would be okay.

There was a gentle tug on her arm. Celine glanced to her side, noticing her daughter's worried expression. She knelt down to her level. "What is it, sweetie?"

"Will Tucker be okay?"

"I'm sure she will be fine."

"You look sad and need a hug." Savannah leaned forward and wrapped her arms around her mother's neck. "I love you, Mommy."

"Oh sweetheart, I love you, too. And yes, I need a long hug to forget whatever else is happening around us," Celine uttered, blinking back tears.

The fire department's battalion chief approached her. "Ma'am, I understand this is your home?"

Tears threatened to fall, but she held it together. "Yes. How bad is it?"

"The kitchen suffered the worst of it. The living room has some damage. Our crew knocked down the fire quickly. There's smoke damage on the first floor and the kitchen will have to undergo a major remodel."

"How did it start?"

"Unknown at this time. Once it cools off, our investigator will conduct his investigation to determine the ignition point."

"What about the bedrooms?" Celine asked.

"The upstairs is untouched. But you won't be able to live in it until the debris is cleared, the inspection is finished, and repairs are completed. If you don't have family or somewhere to stay tonight, the Red Cross can arrange a hotel for you." He waved over a Red Cross volunteer to where they stood.

"Hello, ma'am. I'm Caroline. I'm going to guide you on what steps you'll need to take from here on."

"This is devastating. I don't know what to do, where to go with my daughter," Celine said in shock.

"We can put you up in a hotel for a few nights until you figure out your living arrangements," the volunteer advised.

Celine hated the thought of the upheaval to Savannah's life, but they had no other choice.

A firefighter taking a water break overheard them talking

and glanced their way. "Celine?"

She recognized him. "Anthony! Is it bad?"

"You'll need a new kitchen and living room."

"Oh, God."

Anthony reached into his pocket and pulled out several business cards for contractors and cleaning services that specialize in smoke damage. "These businesses are trustworthy and do good work. Call them. They'll take good care of you."

"Thank you," she said, looking over the cards in her hand. "Not the way I envisioned spending the holidays."

"Are there family or friends you can stay with while your place gets cleaned up?"

"Unfortunately, no. We'll make do in a hotel."

Anthony paused a long moment. "I have a small cottage—an in-law setup—in my backyard. I had planned to rent it out, but hadn't got around to it yet. You can stay in it if you like."

Celine opened her mouth to protest, and Anthony stopped her.

"Stay in the hotel the Red Cross is offering. Just for tonight. Tomorrow, after I'm off duty, I can show you the cottage. Then you can decide if it will work for you. Call Bridget if you're having any thoughts or concerns about me or the place."

She wasn't entirely sure it was a good idea.

"It isn't anything fancy, but you won't have to pay for a hotel in the city. Besides, it's only until your place is livable. And I won't charge you rent."

"I don't want to impose."

"Consider it my Christmas goodwill." Anthony looked down at Savannah. The sadness on her face tore at his heart. "Really, it's fine. My cottage will give you your own space. And with the holiday hotel bookings, it may be your only option."

This was Bridget's brother offering. "Okay."

"I'll take you inside so you can get what you need."

They waited until the battalion chief gave the all clear. Savannah stayed outside with a neighbor while Anthony escorted her inside. Celine stepped into the house and stopped. She let out a long sigh and looked around in shock. Her beautiful kitchen stood in ruins. An inch of water pooled on the floor. The putrid smell of smoke invaded her sinuses and caused her to cough. Her life had changed drastically in an instant. A catastrophe she never imagined. If she were a weaker woman, she would have fallen into a heap on the floor and cried.

But Celine would never do that. For her daughter, she would remain strong. She would summon the courage to deal with the nightmare they found themselves in. There was no other choice.

He took her elbow and led her upstairs to gather things she would need over the next few weeks.

The bedrooms appeared to be fine. Thankfully, the doors were closed and escaped any smoke damage. Tucker meowed when she opened the door to Savannah's bedroom. She had left the window open, which allowed fresh air into the room.

Celine pulled out two suitcases and shoved clothing, shoes, and toiletries into them. After putting Tucker into her cat carrier, they went back outside and got the hotel details from the Red Cross volunteer.

8

After a restless night at the hotel, Celine and Savannah met Anthony at his place. After talking with Bridget, Celine decided to stay at Anthony's cottage. He took Celine's two suitcases from her and brought them inside and set them down in the living room. He flicked on the light. "Come inside where it's warm."

Celine wiped her feet on the doormat before stepping inside and setting down the cat carrier. Tucker protested loudly at being confined in the small carrier. Savannah followed closely behind, wearing her school backpack over her shoulders and carrying a beloved stuffed animal.

Anthony turned toward Celine and Savannah in the cozy guest cottage to gauge their reaction. "You'll need this." He handed Celine a set of keys.

Savannah reached up to hold her mother's hand, her small fingers wrapping around Celine's as they looked around. There were comfortable furnishings. A dark-blue sofa sat in front of the fireplace, and two matching recliners stood to the side. A flat screen television engulfed the space over the fireplace. The room displayed no pictures or personal things. The cottage was a significant improvement from the hotel they stayed in.

This is home now, she reminded herself, content with the arrangement. And it was comforting to know they would still be in the same neighborhood, close to Savannah's school and daycare if repairs to her home took longer than expected.

Anthony ran a hand down the stubble on his face, preferring not to shave on his days off from the firehouse. "Well, what do you think?"

"Your cottage is lovely. We appreciate you letting us stay here. Although I must insist on giving you something to cover the electricity and water bill."

"That won't be necessary."

"Where's my bedroom?" Savannah asked, her curiosity sparked.

Kneeling down at her level from his towering height, Anthony grinned at her enthusiasm. "There are two bedrooms. You and your mother can decide which one you'd like to sleep in."

Savannah enthusiastically explored every room, her bright eyes wide with inquisitiveness.

"We're treating this as a big adventure. It helps to soften the blow of all the upheaval in her life," Celine said.

He gave Celine a tour and showed her where fresh sheets and towels were stored. "The Wi-Fi password is on a notepad on the front of the refrigerator. If you need anything else, just let me know."

Celine took in the cottage. It was as comfortable and cozy as a bed-and-breakfast inn. There was a sense of calmness that filled her, knowing Savannah felt comfortable with the living arrangement. "How is it a man can make his cottage so warm and inviting? My brother's idea of decor is a neon beer light above a mini fridge next to his pool table and collection of beer steins."

He lowered his head and stood quietly for a few moments.

Clearly, she'd hit a nerve of some kind. "I'm sorry. I didn't mean to pry."

He met her eyes. "My wife decorated the place."

He's married?

Her eyes went round. "Your wife?"

"I'm a widower."

Celine swallowed. "I'm sorry. I had no idea."

"A drunk driver hit her car. It was a long time ago."

His words hung in the air. An awkward ease settled over them. She understood loss and how it felt as if a part of you was missing. "How awful. Sudden loss is incredibly tough." Her heart ached for him. She reached out and ran a hand down his arm in a comforting gesture. "If you ever need a friend to talk to about her, I'm a good listener."

"Thanks. I appreciate it."

Celine bit her lip with a worried frown and raised her gaze. "And you're sure you don't mind the cat here?"

"The cat is fine."

"We'll make sure she doesn't do any damage. After we unpack, we're heading out to the grocery store for some food. Can I pick you up anything?" she asked.

"I'm stocked up. But thanks for asking."

"Thank you, Anthony. I can't tell you how much we appreciate you letting us stay here. We'll take good care of the place."

She watched him walk across the lawn to his house and made a mental note to call Bridget later and tell her what a great brother she has. His kindness and offer of letting them stay in his cottage gave her a lot less to worry about. She'd have to think of something nice to do for him to show her appreciation.

9

Boxes were lined up on the front lawn. The rocking chair that Celine used to rock Savannah to sleep as a baby stood nearby. A neighbor brought a plastic bin to help contain the items, and in it, she neatly stacked photo albums.

Celine looked through her belongings in the front yard, things the firefighters saved. She pulled out another box and looked through it, checking for any damage to the contents. She got caught up in rifling through the items, desperately trying to find the scrapbook of Dex she'd made for Savannah.

She thought of when she and Dex moved into their house. They'd made the old worn out house into a warm and loving home. For so long, it had been Celine and Dex. Then, when Savannah arrived, they'd become a family in this house. There were so many memories of their time in this home. It hurt when she looked at it and all she saw was destruction.

For the first time in months, Celine felt lost and adrift. She missed Dex and wished he were here with her. But he wasn't and never would be again. She had done her best to help Savannah deal with the loss of her father. And now, everything had changed again so suddenly.

What brought her back to her reality and made her face the tragedy was her daughter. Celine had no choice but to be strong for Savannah and help her with the situation resulting from the fire at their home. The upheaval of their lives made her realize she needed to step up and move forward. Make every moment with Savannah count.

Her grief for her old life would always be inside her. Being married, waking up with her husband, having family dinners with Savannah...such was the life she mourned. The life she struggled to make sense of and move past.

Tears stung the back of Celine's eyes.

"Can I help?"

The familiar voice had Celine glancing up to find Bridget standing beside her, searching her face with concern.

"Anthony told me you would be here. If I can help, I'm here for you."

"I don't know where to start," Celine choked out. "They saved my photo albums, which were important. The only other thing I really want to find is a scrapbook of Dex. It means a lot to Savannah."

"I'll help you look."

Celine hugged her friend. It was a relief to have someone here to help. With her family living in Connecticut, she had no other relatives to turn to. "There's a storage shed in the backyard. I'll store everything there until the remodel is finished." She picked up a couple of boxes and went to the backyard.

Bridget found Celine a few minutes later crying. In her hand she held the broken pieces of a hummingbird feeder.

"Savannah and I made it after Dex died. She was having nightmares after seeing a news clip about the incident on the news. I wanted her to feel safe."

The meaning of the hummingbird wasn't lost on Bridget.

She handed Celine a box stained with soot and ash. "The remnants of the Christmas garden. Anthony boxed it up the night of the fire. All it needs is a good cleaning and Savannah can display all her treasures again in her garden."

Celine held back the tears threatening to fall. "Thank you."

"I think I found it," Celine said out loud as she pulled a large scrapbook from another box of belongings. Along with it was a handcrafted wooden box. "It's in good shape and doesn't smell like smoke." When she opened it, she was speechless, staring at all the military medals and police award medals inside.

Celine had loaded a few of the boxes of belongings into her car and brought them back to the cottage to go through. Finding Dex's belongings was imperative, and now a heavy weight lifted from her shoulders.

"Mommy, what are those?" Savannah asked, peering into the box.

Celine sat down on the floor with Savannah and held open the box. "These are some of Daddy's treasured possessions. Your daddy was a hero. He saved lives not only the day he went to heaven, but several other times as well."

"I miss him."

"Oh, sweetie, Daddy will always be with you in your heart, right here." She took Savannah's hand and placed it on her chest. "When you're afraid of anything, talk to Daddy. He can hear your prayers. Daddy loved you more than anything."

That night after Savannah had a bath and went to bed, Celine put on her slippers and tip-toed down the hall, opening the bedroom door, and stood there listening to Savannah's soft breathing. She was sleeping peacefully.

After the turmoil of the fire, having to pack their bags and temporarily move, Savannah seemed to take the changes to their lives in stride. Celine never had been more proud of her than now.

Living as a single mother was hard work. Celine had struggled at first, figuring out how to live without Dex. He had always been supportive of her and they worked well as a team. She missed him, but was learning how to manage without him. They would make it through this tough life lesson and come out stronger. Celine was more determined than ever to give her daughter a life she so deserved.

She went to bed soon after, crawling under the blankets, exhausted. But sleep would not come easy for her tonight, and her thoughts went to Dex. She lay awake imagining what her life would be like if Dex were still alive and they were going about their daily lives. He had wanted another baby, so Savannah would have a sibling. He was a great father, always making time for his daughter no matter what else in life was happening. Memories of Dex flooded her mind—when she met him, their wedding, how happy he was when Savannah was born. There were so many moments to cherish she would never forget.

I will always love you, Dex.

At some point, Celine drifted off to sleep, and her dreams filled with images of her husband and the life they once had.

10

Anthony stood at his window and watched Celine place the Christmas wreath on the front door, and on each side of the entryway she placed a pair of poinsettia plants. She stood back and admired her work before returning inside. He understood it wasn't home and their circumstances were overwhelming, but Celine tried to make it comforting and festive for Savannah.

He shrugged on his jacket and headed for the cottage. A young girl's laughter filled his ears before Savannah opened the door with her mother right behind her. "I hope I'm not interrupting."

"Hi, Anthony," Savannah greeted him. "Did you smell the cookies Mommy and I are baking?"

A big smile lit up his face, the sweet voice wrapping around him, warm and welcoming. The smell of apples and cinnamon wafted around him, bringing memories of a childhood Christmas. "Whatever you're baking smells great." The scent tantalized his nose and his mouth watered with anticipation, hoping they planned to share.

"Hello, Anthony," Celine said, stepping forward.

It was impossible to tell what was more distracting—the sweets, or the woman standing in front of him. It didn't matter. He liked both.

"When you were out earlier, I fixed the light over the front door. You don't have to worry about coming home in the dark now."

"I appreciate it. I also wanted to thank you for saving the photo albums from my house. They're irreplaceable."

"I'm happy they didn't sustain any water damage. Thankfully, the fire wasn't as bad as it could have been."

He glanced between them and couldn't help but notice they wore matching outfits. Each wearing the same red Christmas sweater with a large picture of Santa Claus covering the front. His gaze moved down Celine's long legs covered by faded jeans and they stopped at the red candy cane striped socks on her feet. "Cute socks," he said, amused.

"We like to embrace the holiday spirit. Come inside. We're making cookies," she said, gesturing for him to follow her.

The buzz of activity drew him inside, his eyes pouring over the festive decorations. "Where is my kitchen and what have you done with it? Am I in Santa's kitchen?"

Christmas music played throughout the room. Sparkling twinkle lights hung over the cabinets, giving the kitchen the right amount of festive cheer. A miniature Christmas tree full of ornaments and lights stood on the counter.

The coziness and comfort of their Christmas spirit touched a nerve. It reminded him of when he was a child and his mother was alive. When Anthony, Bridget, Rob, and Christian would help their mother make cookies in their kitchen.

Savannah giggled. "We're making Christmas cookies!"

"I see that."

"Our Christmas tradition," Celine added.

"Want to help?" Savannah asked with a bright smile and cheerful enthusiasm, typical for a child during the holiday season. "We're making my daddy's favorite cookies, peanut blossoms. We make these and sugar cookies and gingerbread men."

On the counter sat a cluster of pastry bags twisted with different colors of icing. Scattered across every surface of the kitchen were mixing bowls, containers full of red and green sprinkles, and cookie sheets filled with cookies ready to go into the oven.

Anthony circled the kitchen table where baked cookies were cooling. He wanted to taste each one. "Do you need a taste-tester? I happen to be available for the job."

Savannah handed him a napkin, holding a gingerbread man she made.

He took a bite, and the flavors exploded in his mouth. "Mmm, this is delicious."

Savannah smiled.

"Miss Savannah, your cookies are so much better than my sister's. Her gingerbread men are usually missing a head."

Savannah doubled over, giggling. "I have a secret to tell you. You can't tell anyone."

"You can tell me anything. I won't tell a soul. Scout's honor." Anthony held up the three-finger salute.

"I have a friend who is one of Santa's elves!" Savannah went on to tell him all about *Teddy* and how he lived in the tree over her holiday garden. "Some of the toys in the garden got dirty from the ash from our house fire. Mommy and I are going to wash the toys and put them back in the garden soon to make everyone happy again."

"I'm sure Teddy will be thrilled. You're a lucky little girl to have an elf for a friend."

"He's my best friend!"

Celine brewed fresh coffee, then put another batch of cookies into the oven. She turned and handed him a mug of the fresh brew along with a smile. "Cheers, Anthony."

And then he smiled back. A warmth grew within his chest. His body hummed with awareness. Visions of this woman in his arms, with his lips covering hers, sprang to life. Moisture dampened the back of his neck as other thoughts ran through his mind.

Thoughts that were wrong on so many levels.

He knew he should move away from her and go back to his house. Her life seemed complicated enough without him coming on to her. But she seemed so sweet, so loving with her daughter, and there was an attraction he was fighting hard for the woman in front of him. A woman he could get used to seeing every day.

He pushed that thought to the side.

Celine finished eating a cookie and offered him another.

"Are you looking to put me in a sugar coma?"

"We can't eat them all. Otherwise, I won't fit into my clothes." She focused back on the cookies, pulling a batch from the oven and busied herself with a spatula, placing the cookies on the paper towels placed on the counter. After she put another batch into the oven, she turned toward Anthony. What she saw in his eyes made her heart stutter. "Why are you looking at me like that?"

His eyes held mischief and heat. "You missed a spot." He reached out and wiped his thumb over her bottom lip, removing a speck of icing. Stared into her eyes for an awkward moment. She was so close.

He wanted to kiss her.

That was for another time, another place.

The oven buzzer broke the spell between them. She turned on her heels to remove the last batch of cookies from the oven. "I'm sending you home with some."

Anthony wasn't about to disagree. "Only not too many. You wouldn't believe how many people bring cookies down to the firehouse for us."

11

With a worried sigh, Celine stepped from her car and moved to Savannah's classroom. Bridget had called her and asked Celine to meet after the school day ended to discuss a disruption during class that Savannah had instigated.

Celine stepped inside the classroom unprepared to learn about her daughter's behavior that day.

With a resigned sigh, Bridget pulled Celine aside and told her about the incident during class.

Celine's mouth gaped. She'd had no behavior issues with Savannah before. But with the house fire and the disruption of their temporary move, combined with Savannah's intense longing for her father, her outburst in class did not surprise her. Celine told Bridget about Dex. "She's having a hard time this year missing her father."

"I have a feeling this has to do with the holiday father-daughter dance more than the fire you endured. I distributed the flyers before the incident occurred. She seemed stressed and became quite teary," Bridget told her.

They sat down with Savannah, and Celine addressed her. "Miss Callahan told me you had a tough moment in class today."

"I miss Daddy." Savannah gazed up at her mother with

eyes filled with sadness.

"I know you do, sweetie. I do, too."

Tears welled in Savannah's eyes. "I wish Daddy was here to take me to the dance."

Celine looked down at her daughter and felt like crying herself. Nothing was going right. Her husband wasn't here, the fire destroyed her kitchen, and her daughter was going through her own hard felt grief over their losses. Sometimes it was too much for one person to handle alone.

A twinge of guilt moved through her. She couldn't feel sorry for herself. She had to pull herself together, buck up, be there for Savannah. Even though her own heart was breaking, Celine couldn't afford to fall apart. Savannah needed her to be strong. And so she would. This incident was only one setback. She'd keep pushing forward, no matter how hard it seemed. She inhaled a deep breath.

"Anything I can do to help?" Bridget asked.

"This is the first father-daughter dance for her. Losing her father was painfully difficult."

"I know about losing a parent, although I wasn't as young as Savannah."

"I'm not sure what to do. Are moms allowed to sub for a dad?"

"Is there someone who could take her? Do you have a brother or relative nearby?"

Celine shook her head. "My family is on the East Coast."

"What about a boyfriend?"

"I don't date." When Celine saw her face, she elaborated. "If a man entered her life and, up and left, it could leave Savannah emotionally scarred."

"I understand your reasoning."

"I'm not ready to date. I don't know if I ever will be. Her father was such an important part of our lives. Since Dex died, I'm having a hard time moving forward. All I've ever done is make sure Savannah is okay."

Bridget asked Savannah to get a book across the room to distract her. When she was out of earshot, Bridget leaned forward and spoke in a low voice. "Maybe it's time to take care of yourself. You're still young. Keep your heart open. You never know when you'll get another chance at love."

Celine shook her head. "I have no desire to date anyone."

"I have three single brothers. You already know Anthony. I'd love to introduce you to Christian and Rob."

Her eyes widened. "Don't you dare."

"I don't know if Anthony told you, but he lost his wife several years ago. Losing her broke my brother. He struggled, and it took him a long time to come to terms with his wife being gone. Gradually, he let go of the hold that had crushed his heart. It wasn't easy for him to move forward. At first, it was hard for him to date, but he realized he doesn't want to be alone the rest of his life."

"I understand loneliness."

Bridget turned to her with a glimmer in her eyes. "He asked me about you. I think he wants to spend some time with you, but wasn't sure if you would be receptive." Bridget noted the way Celine's expression changed when she mentioned Anthony.

"Honestly, I'm scared to move forward. I've thought about it, but I have to think about Savannah first." Maybe one day in the future she'd consider dating.

"My brother is a good guy. Anthony is the kind of man you waited your entire life to meet, even though you had no idea you were waiting." Bridget lifted her left brow. "Think about it. Seriously, think about it."

"I'll admit, your brother is easy on the eyes. But that's all I'm saying. Don't think about playing matchmaker."

Bridget reached out and gave her arm a quick squeeze. "Give him a chance. What could it hurt?"

Celine waved off Bridget's attempt at matchmaking with a shake of her head. It was time to escape the subject of her love life. "We'll figure this out."

Savannah stepped in front of Bridget and held up a book. "May I please borrow this book and take it home to read?"

"You certainly may."

Celine stood. "We should go. Thanks for the pep talk."

"See you at the dance."

Before Celine was even out the door, Bridget called Anthony.

"I know she's interested. But she won't admit it. She's afraid to take that first step."

"Don't push her. It took me some time to let go of the *brooding widower* and embrace life again."

"Lily would have agreed that you'd mourned long enough. You deserve some happiness again in your life."

"Now I just have to convince a certain woman to take a chance on me."

Bridget was certain everything would work out just the way it was supposed to.

Celine had to figure out a way to help Savannah get through the holiday season before she thought about herself. Once they returned to the cottage, she had an idea.

"We've had some upheaval in our lives recently. I know what would make us feel better. Let's put your Christmas garden back together to bring some happiness to our home while it misses us. Then we can come back here and make a pie and bring it to the nice firemen who saved our house."

And that suggestion was all Savannah needed to push away the gloom.

12

Celine and Savannah showing up at the firehouse door surprised Anthony. Celine held a pie in one hand and a tub of ice cream in the other.

"We brought some dessert to thank your crew for saving our house," Celine said.

He ushered her inside, having a hard time keeping his eyes off her. She was wearing black leggings and a soft gray sweater. Miniature Christmas tree earrings hung from her ears and red socks with candy canes covered her feet, tucked inside ballet slippers. She looked beautiful and sexier than any woman he'd ever seen.

Savannah tugged at Anthony's arm. "Anthony! My garden has more gifts to share. Someone left a Polly Pocket!"

Anthony chuckled at her excitement. "You started the sharing garden and I bet a lot of little kids are enjoying it."

"We had to clean it up a bit, but Mommy and I put it back together."

"That's great news."

They went inside the kitchen, and she set down the pie.

"Thank you for the dessert," he said, taking the ice cream from her and putting it inside the freezer. "How did you know pie and ice cream are our favorite?"

"I thought you'd have eaten enough cookies and would like something different."

"Thank you. We appreciate it."

"Anthony," Savannah said in a serious tone. "How come you don't have a Christmas tree?"

"We keep it in the office. The guys I work with can sometimes rough house like ten-year-old boys and we wouldn't want them to break any of the ornaments."

He didn't want to tell her he didn't particularly enjoy celebrating the holiday. For him, it was a reminder of when his wife died. The night he traded shifts with a work buddy. Not having any children of his own, Anthony typically worked Christmas Eve for one of the guys with kids so they could spend Christmas morning with their family. After they had finished opening gifts, his work buddy would come in to work around noon, and Anthony would go off to spend the day with his family.

He still carried the guilt of not being with Lily the night of the accident, that Christmas Eve she ventured to her sister's home while he worked. Anthony hadn't enjoyed Christmas since that day.

"Let's go see the tree. I'm sure there's a candy cane on it for you."

After getting Savannah's expert opinion on their Christmas tree and letting her sit in one of the firetrucks pretending to be a firefighter, Celine said it was time to go. Anthony walked them outside and said goodbye.

As he was venturing back inside, he looked over his shoulder, watching them leave, and caught sight of one of the neighborhood beat cops parked in the lot and stepping from his patrol car.

"Celine, is that you?" the cop called out.

She glanced over to find Matt Franklin moving toward her.

He immediately sent her a big smile and caught her in his

arms, and gave her a long hug. "It's so good to see you, Celine. What are you doing here?"

"Visiting a friend."

Matt shot a quick glance at Anthony at the door before turning his undivided attention back to Celine. "How have you and Savannah been?"

Celine half shrugged. "Surviving." The gloom in her tone came through clearly.

"I'm sorry about your house."

"It's bittersweet. I'm getting the new kitchen I always wanted."

"Other than that, are you doing okay?"

Matt and Dex were partners when Dex was a rookie. They had worked together for years and had been good friends.

"We're doing fine," she said.

"I don't see enough of you and Savannah anymore. I'm not sure how you feel about this, but would you like to have dinner with me sometime?"

"Matt, I'd love to. But it's not a good time right now. Savannah is going through a rough patch, still having a hard time dealing with Dex gone. Maybe once she's not so clingy we could get together. Since the fire, my life has been a mess."

"When your life calms down, we'll have that dinner. Let's stay in touch."

"I'd like that." The words slipped out of her mouth easily.

Matt watched her walk away and turned back to the firehouse. He noted Anthony standing in the doorway. Their eyes met and held, as if they were each trying to figure out each other's relationship with Celine.

A pang of jealousy stirred deep in Anthony's gut as he observed them.

"Hey, Callahan," Franklin called out in greeting, moving toward the door.

Anthony lifted his chin before going back into the

firehouse. He ignored Franklin mostly, having never been particularly fond of the guy.

Anthony had watched their exchange. Franklin and Celine obviously knew each other. The way she had smiled at him made Anthony feel as if a dagger had pierced his heart. He sucked in a breath. Faced with his feelings and now having competition, he had to suck it up and deal with it. He had no claim on her. They'd had coffee.

Once.

But there were other things about Franklin he wasn't sure Celine knew about.

Franklin came into the kitchen and poured himself a cup of coffee. The guys at the firehouse always kept a fresh pot on. Franklin dug in his wallet, pulled out a dollar bill, and put it into the coffee donation jar next to the coffeepot.

In order to keep the rivalry between the fire department and police department at bay and to maintain harmony within both departments, the beat cops were always welcome to stop by, write their reports, and have a cup.

Franklin sat down beside Anthony at the kitchen table. "How ya doing, Callahan?"

"Be doing better if I hadn't witnessed you putting the moves on her."

"We're old friends. I worked with her husband."

"So now that he's gone, you think you're going to replace him?"

Franklin sat back in his chair. "What's it to you?"

"Looking out for a friend. Maybe you should give her some space."

"Who she sees isn't any of your business."

"I'm making it my business."

"It's like that, huh?" Franklin leered at him.

Anthony leered back at the man. Franklin was as tall as Anthony, but not as well built. Hardly a threat. "Damn right it is."

"I thought we'd moved past that bad blood between us."

"Stay away from her. I'd hate for her to learn about what went on between you and your ex. I'm sure she wouldn't feel the same way about you knowing what you're capable of."

The air crackled with tension, adversaries sizing each other up. Battle lines drawn.

Anthony never liked the guy and didn't want him anywhere near Celine.

The man who showed up at a bar with a woman who was not his girlfriend. Anthony and a few of his friends were playing pool in the back. He noticed Franklin at the bar, drinking with the woman, doing shots.

Anthony's co-worker, Ty, who was playing pool with him, also noticed what Anthony was focused on after glancing over. Ty's eyes locked on Franklin as he did a shot. He watched Franklin for a moment, trying to contain himself and not beat the man to a bloody pulp. Ty's sister had been dating Franklin for six months and they were getting serious, already talking about moving in together and getting married.

Franklin had the bartender line up several more shots on the bar. He pushed half toward the woman, who shook her head, refusing to drink more. He knocked one back and turned toward her. Obviously drunk, Franklin raised his brows in that way he had that said, *No one tells me no.* He insisted the woman take another shot. When she refused, he grabbed her arm, twisting it until she cried out in pain. As he lifted his other hand as if he would strike her, Ty grabbed his arm to stop him. Franklin shoved him, sending Ty back a step, then Franklin lunged for the woman. "See what you did! Now take the fucking shot!"

The bar brawl ensued.

It took three men to pull Franklin away from her and a

good old-fashioned ass whooping from Ty to send a message about how to treat women. They held him down until the cops arrived. The woman declined to press charges, so Franklin suffered no consequences other than losing the respect of the entire firehouse.

Since that incident, the guys treated him as an outcast and all around jerk.

While on duty, they had to respond to the same calls occasionally. Anthony remained professional at work only because he had to.

"I ever see you lay a hand on another woman, I promise you, you'll have to be wheeled into jail," Anthony growled, pushed back his chair, and walked away.

He wasn't bluffing.

13

Celine pulled the curtains open to look outside and see what type of day to expect. Winters in San Francisco were generally mild, but a storm lingered off the coast, expected to make landfall within the next few days. Noting the sway of the branches in the trees told her the storm could be early.

Her eyes caught sight of Anthony across the yard. He certainly was an early riser and go-getter. He stood on a ladder resting against the back of his house, doing something to the roof's gutters. She stood at the window, surprised by the pleasure she felt watching him.

Most definitely easy on the eyes.

She had felt nothing like that in a long time.

How is this man not with a woman every night?

Taking a deep breath, she pushed the brakes on any racy thoughts. Don't even go there. Not going to happen. Since Dex passed, she hadn't even looked at another man.

Until now.

Savannah distracted her by asking for breakfast, and she turned to go back into the kitchen. "What would you like? We can make pancakes and bacon."

A loud bang from outside shook the ground. Was that an earthquake?

Opening the door, a groan echoed from the yard. The metal ladder lay on the ground, with Anthony sprawled beside it. She reacted on instinct and ran toward him.

Blood was the first thing she noticed. Bright red streaks running down Anthony's arm. She noted the military ink on his corded forearm. If he was like her brothers who served, he'd never admit to any pain. She couldn't help but wince before making eye contact. "You're bleeding. Are you okay?"

"Other than my bruised ego running away with my manhood, I'm fine."

"What were you doing?"

He sat up. "I thought it was time to stop being the grinch and put up some Christmas lights. A gust of wind sent a broken branch my way in a direct hit."

"Let me look," she said, reaching for him.

He straightened his arm out, exposing the jagged edges of a bloody wound that curved around his left arm.

Nice biceps.

Very muscular biceps.

Her breath caught as her fingers touched his arm, and it was enough to send a bolt of electricity through her. Suddenly, it felt warm.

Outside.

In the cold.

Anthony flicked his cool blue eyes to her. "It's just a scratch."

"Hardly."

"Don't tell anyone I fell off the ladder. Especially my sister. I'll never live it down. Firefighters don't fall off ladders." He grinned and creases fan at his eyes.

The playful expression on his face made her lose her train of thought.

"Celine."

The deep timbre of his voice jarred her back to the present, out of her thoughts, and she looked into his face. "Your secret is safe with me," she said, unable to suppress a smile.

"I certainly hope so. My siblings can be brutal."

"With two older brothers, I understand how it is with siblings." She paused a moment. "I'll be right back. There's a first aid kit in the kitchen."

She returned minutes later and forced herself to concentrate on the task at hand. After she cleaned his arm with some sterile saline, she got a good look at the wound and gave her opinion. "You need stitches."

"I've got super glue. Works just as well," he countered.

She sent him a look. "That jagged edge on the ladder looks rusty. You should get a round of antibiotics."

"You're a nurse. Can you stitch me up?"

"I can. But you should see a doctor and get a tetanus shot."

"Just fix me up enough so I don't bleed out."

Her hair caught in the breeze, and he brushed it from her eyes.

She met his gaze and paused a beat. "Let's go inside."

Celine washed her hands at the sink, donned a pair of sterile gloves, and pulled suture materials from her medical kit. He sat in front of her at the kitchen table, studying the slice on his arm. She applied a topical pain reducing medication and disinfected the wound area with an anti-bacterial antiseptic solution.

"Are you scared?" Celine asked.

"I trust you."

She took a quick glance at his face. "This may hurt some."

He leveled dreamy blue eyes at her and grinned. "I can handle it."

Anthony didn't seem worried about any pain, which made her relax. When she poked him with the needle, he didn't even flinch. Focusing on the wound, she worked in silence, concentrating on looping the needle and thread in and out of his skin. The only sound came from the cartoons on the television Savannah watched in the living room.

Feeling his eyes wash over her, she glanced at him. She wasn't wrong. His heated eyes were focused on her. Being this close to him, smelling his woodsy scent, made her slightly uncomfortable. It also made her fantasize about what it would be like being even closer. She quickly brushed that thought away.

"You're good. Doesn't hurt a bit."

Minutes later, she tied off the last suture and cut the thread. "Five stitches. The scar should be minimal."

He bent his head to look closer. She could smell his hair. Vanilla. Nice.

"You still need to go to the hospital for a shot," she reminded him as she covered the wound with a bandage.

"I hate hospitals."

"Suck it up, tough guy, and get your shot." She moved to stand in front of him. "I appreciate you being a good patient and not squirming like most I deal with."

"And I appreciate you stitching me up. If you're done torturing me, I'll go get that shot." He smiled at her and something shifted between them. "Thanks for this."

Celine packed up her medical kit and could sense his reluctancy to leave. "Why don't you come over for dinner tonight? I'm making beef stew, Savannah's favorite meal."

His eyes locked on hers. "I won't argue with that. She isn't the only one fond of beef stew. Can I bring anything?"

"Just yourself. Dinner's at six."

14

The small kitchen smelled like beef stew and freshly baked bread. Savannah set the table and put the cat's food in her dish. Celine lifted the cover off the pot and gave the stew one last stir, satisfied it had simmered long enough. Dinner was ready. She pulled the homemade sourdough bread from the oven and smiled proudly as she turned to her daughter. "You did a great job with the bread. It smells delicious."

Celine loved teaching Savannah to cook. They often baked all of Dex's favorite cookies and casseroles as something to do together to keep his spirit alive. Over dinner, they would often talk about him, and Celine would tell stories of her life with Dex before Savannah was born.

"When is Anthony coming over? I'm hungry," Savannah said.

Moments later, the doorbell chimed.

"That must be him now."

"Something smells delicious." Anthony stood at the door with a grin and handed a bottle of wine to Celine.

He followed her into the kitchen. Celine retrieved a pair of wineglasses and Anthony opened the wine, pouring two glasses while she sliced the sourdough bread.

During dinner, Savannah regaled Anthony with tales of

Teddy the elf, his letters he wrote her, and the treasures she had left in her Christmas garden. Celine found herself transfixed by the way he listened to her and was so attentive to Savannah.

Why would he still be single? A good-looking man like him who has a sweet way with kids?

Celine rarely entertained at home, most certainly not with men. But out of nowhere, under the strangest of circumstances, she'd met Anthony, and it was so clear on some level, whether or not she understood it, that they belonged together as friends. She connected with him in a way she hadn't felt with anyone before. And tonight, she thoroughly enjoyed herself.

Anthony's deep voice drew her from her thoughts. His attention had returned to her. All six plus feet of him.

When she gazed into his deep blue eyes, her cheeks flushed. She took in his handsome face with its strong jawline, and once more her gaze settled on his eyes. "I'm sorry. What did you say?"

"I was telling Savannah that I had a surprise for her."

Savannah's eyes lit up. "I like surprises."

"You'll like this one. Now that it's dark, you can see it. Let's go outside."

They followed him outside and Savannah squealed in delight, staring at the two houses in wonder. "It looks like Christmas!"

Brightly colored Christmas lights trimmed each house. Anthony also strung lights on the shrubs.

"I had some help from my crew from the firehouse."

They stood together as they watched Savannah dance in the glow of the Christmas lights. Celine spontaneously wrapped her arms around him. "Thank you." Tears welled in her eyes. "What you've done for Savannah is so sweet and overwhelming."

"Children need to believe in hope, goodness, and love. She deserves this. I never thought I'd say this, but I'm actually looking forward to Christmas."

Celine raised her eyes to his and saw compassion. "You are the sweetest man I know." She wanted to reach out and touch his freshly shaven face. Had the strong urge to kiss him. Before she realized what she was doing, she reached up and placed both hands on his face and kissed him on the cheek with a gentleness that spun from her heart.

"Mommy, look!" Savannah smiled wide and her eyes filled with wonder. She pointed out the lighted Santa and reindeer display on top of the roof.

Anthony's arm wrapped around her shoulders and gave her a gentle squeeze. Celine welcomed the affectionate contact. She'd missed the feeling of a man's touch. It was all she could do to resist dropping her head to rest on his broad shoulder. If there was ever a time that she thought he could steal her heart, it was at this moment.

They went back into the house, and Savannah's mood changed. The smile she had on her face morphed into a frown.

"Why are you so sad?" Anthony asked. "Don't you like the outside lights?"

Savannah told him about her school's daddy-daughter dance and how she couldn't go.

Tenderness filled his eyes. "Why not?"

"My daddy is in heaven."

"When is the dance?"

"Friday night."

He paused a beat. "I have an idea. I'm not your father, but do you think he'd mind if I took you to the dance?"

Savannah's eyes widened. "You'll go with me?"

"If it's all right with your mother."

Celine inclined her head. "I'd hate for us to take you away

from your other obligations. Don't you have a girlfriend who would mind?"

"No girlfriend."

She swallowed.

No girlfriend.

"I'm sure you have other things to do other than take a little girl to a dance."

"It will be a pleasure to take Savannah. I haven't been to a dance with a pretty girl in years."

His charming smile sent goosebumps up and down her arms.

"That's so sweet. I don't know what to say." Celine smiled, and he sent her a wink.

"Say yes."

She nodded. There was no denying the man was not only attractive, but kind and generous with his time. If she was honest with herself, she wouldn't mind dancing in his arms, either.

After Celine tucked Savannah in bed, she came back into the room and observed Anthony facing the tree as if lost in thought. His expression puzzled her. "You don't really like Christmas, do you?"

Aware that she was watching him, he turned toward her and caught her eye. "What makes you think so?"

"Christmas is a state of mind. Warm and fuzzy feelings, and I don't see you feeling it at the moment."

He paused, surprised at how perceptive she was. Anthony never talked about his wife much to anyone other than his sister.

"I can tell you love the holidays," he said in response, hoping to avoid *that* conversation.

"I love Christmas. If for nothing other than my daughter to

feel the love and goodwill. I'm sure there are a lot of reasons for some people not to feel the same way. If I'm being too nosey, tell me."

He rubbed the back of his neck and closed his eyes for a moment. "My wife died in a car accident on Christmas Eve. I was supposed to be with her on her way to her sister's house. But I volunteered to work that night so another firefighter could spend the morning opening gifts with his kids. Instead, Lily drove alone. A drunk driver hit her car. If I'd have been with her, I would have been driving. The way he t-boned her car, he most likely would have killed me. Maybe she would have survived. Luck, fate, I don't know what to call it. I'm still here and she isn't doesn't seem right. All I know is, I wasn't in the car with her when I should have been and she'd probably still be alive. When she died, I blamed myself."

The gravity of his words pulled at her heart. "It's why you avoid Christmas. I'm sorry about your wife." She put her arms around him, feeling his loss profoundly, aching for him. She gently stroked his back to comfort him. "I know how devastating it is to lose someone you love."

"Even as I felt conflicted that my job kept me from being with her that day, I wanted to make sense of it. I threw myself into my job. It took a long time, but work ultimately saved me. I've made peace with her death. Lily would have wanted me to find some happiness out of life and not mourn her forever."

Anthony pulled away from her and met her eyes, and for an instant, Celine could see the raw grief reflected in his gaze. He had lost his wife, and she understood what he felt. She had lost Dex in a horrific tragedy. "We're both navigating our grief the best way we know how. It's all we can do."

"When I saw Savannah's garden, it made me think of Lily. Your little girl made me realize I had to keep pushing forward. Somehow, I had to change how I viewed the holidays. I pushed aside my demons, wanting to bring joy to someone else. Do something to make a little girl happy."

Celine pulled him down to the sofa to sit beside her. "And you did. What a kind heart you have."

He looked at her again. "You being here and listening are a great comfort. I've enjoyed spending time with you both. She's been a bright spot in my life. Writing her notes gave me peace in a horribly painful time of year. I truly needed her as much as she needed Teddy."

"One day when she's older and can understand, I'd like to tell her how her garden helped your outlook."

"Not anytime soon, I hope. I'm still having fun with my *alter ego*."

Celine's expression turned serious. "Can I ask you something personal?"

"Sure."

"How long did you wait after your wife passed before you started dating?"

"At least a year."

"Was it hard? To put yourself back out there?"

"It wasn't easy. My brothers both thought I needed to get back in the game, but my heart wasn't in it. I only went out on a few dates." A mournful silence filled the air for a few moments. Anthony lifted his gaze to hers. "What about you? Have you gone on any dates yet?"

She shook her head. "I haven't been able to bring myself to even think about it. Guilt swallows me up if I do."

"You're a beautiful woman. I can't believe you don't have a long line of men waiting at your door."

"A few have asked me out, but Savannah has been my priority. We're making new traditions without her father." Her eyes dampened when she looked up at him. "I'm sorry." Her hand reached to her face and wiped away a tear.

"You have nothing to be sorry about."

"I brought up things you probably didn't want to talk about. You're also still grieving. And I'm sure you don't want to listen to me go on about Dex."

"Both of us will always grieve the love we lost." His expression softened at the woman who was looking at him with such warmth and empathy. "It's nice to talk to someone who knows where I've been. What I've gone through."

"Does it ever get easier?"

"With time it does."

She stared at him, momentarily mesmerised by his eyes. Anthony leaned forward and wrapped her in his arms, pulling her close. "I want you to feel free to talk to me anytime. You're not alone. Ever."

She dropped her head to his chest and held tight, thinking how natural and comforting it felt to be in his arms. She struggled with that. "I feel guilty thinking about how nice it feels that you're holding me. Honestly, I don't want to move."

"Then don't. I'm here for as long as you need."

"I could stay here forever."

"There's nothing to say that you can't."

When she said nothing, he leaned down and dropped a tender kiss on her head.

Holding her breath, nothing made sense. Celine didn't want to be attracted to him, but she was. Leaning back, she took in his gaze and saw his emotions flickering in his eyes. His warm hand glided up her arm, sending tingling sensations through her chest. She opened her mouth to speak, but he pressed two fingers against her lips to quiet her.

"I want to kiss you," he whispered, pulling her closer.

A battle raged inside her heart. It was both exhilarating and terrifying. She held her breath as she imagined him kissing her, what he'd taste like with his lips covering hers. A gentle kiss between two people who understood each other. Two people who wanted to feel love again.

She hadn't been with anyone since Dex. When he died, she thought she would never be ready to move on.

And then she met Anthony.

For the first time since Dex passed, Celine felt as though her life had turned. She enjoyed the time she spent with Anthony. He was such a good man, an attractive man with a caring heart. And he was interested in her. When he smiled, her heart jumped and her body heated. The thought of being intimate with Anthony was startling and thrilling at once. Celine was a bundle of nerves.

Was she ready to start something so serious? Considering where a kiss could lead, she felt her insides wobble, struggling with her feelings. And then Dex's face filled her mind.

How would Dex feel about them?

She panicked, pulling back and turning away from him. "I can't..." She couldn't find the right words to tell him how wary she was of letting him into her heart, how afraid she was to love again.

Reaching out, he caught her wrist and tugged her back toward him. He leaned forward, closing the distance between them with his face inches from hers. As if he could read her mind, he took her hand and gently squeezed it. "I'm sorry. It was insensitive of me."

She studied him for a few moments. "It's just...I'm not ready for any intimacy. I'm sorry if I led you to believe I was."

He sensed her skittishness stemmed from an underlying guilt and an unspoken vow to honor her deceased husband's memory. His blue gaze searched her face intently. "Don't be sorry, Celine. You did nothing wrong."

"You're not upset?"

"I respect that it's too soon for you."

Her body seemed too aware of him. "I like you. Too much,

if that makes sense."

"And I like you, and your beautiful smile."

She met Anthony's impassioned gaze. There was something in his expression that made her feel more than a little nervous.

He caressed her cheek once more, then let her go and stood. "I should probably get going. Let you get some sleep. Thank you again for dinner."

Celine rose from the sofa, and his arms came around her. He brushed a kiss over her forehead. "Goodnight, Celine."

"Goodnight, Anthony." She watched him walk out the door, but wasn't sure if what they shared was a commiseration of shared losses, or something else. Like loneliness. Or something worse. Attraction.

For the first time in years, she felt attracted to a man who wasn't her husband. She could feel him. A gorgeous, rugged, sexy man who made her want love and tenderness. Ache for something she longed for.

In bed, Celine hugged her pillow and thought of Dex.

I won't ever forget you.

But what if I meet someone and can never fall for them because they aren't you?

What do I do, Dex?

15

Getting Savannah ready for her first dance brought Celine such joy. Savannah had selected a shimmery purple dress with puffy sleeves and a fluffy skirt. The dress was fun and princess-like. She looked beautiful.

"Mommy, are you going to wear a pretty dress like me?"

"I will wear a dress, but it will be nowhere near as beautiful as your dress."

Anthony's expression told a different story when he picked them up to go to the dance. An admiring smile spread over his face as his gaze skimmed down over Celine. A flash of dimples appeared before meeting her eyes with a glimmer. "You both look beautiful."

"I hope you're ready to dance the night away. I haven't seen Savannah this excited for something in months," Celine said.

Anthony leaned over close to her ear. "I hope you'll save me a dance."

She wanted to be bold and take a risk, just as Bridget suggested. Tapping a finger to her lips, she turned toward him. "Only one?"

He grinned.

"Come on. Let's go," Savannah said, lacing her fingers

through Anthony's and tugging him toward the door.

Celine glanced around the room. In many ways, the elementary school gymnasium reminded Celine of her own father-daughter dance she had attended with her father when she was a child. They decorated the room with balloons, colorful streamers, and sparkling strings of fairy lights ran over the doors and windows. A snack table stood against one wall with an array of goodies and treats, along with several punch bowls filled with fruit punch and lemonade.

A steady stream of little girls dressed in their fanciest dresses, walking hand in hand with their *dates,* moved through the enormous space. They all looked so adorable.

Celine's heart swelled as she watched Savannah with her special date. That Anthony asked to escort her to such an important event in a little girl's life warmed her heart. She couldn't admire him much more than she did at this moment when she saw pure joy cover Savannah's face.

Savannah danced and danced with Anthony. After a while, all the little girls took to the snack table. Celine and a few other moms came out of the parents' lounge that was set up for the adults chaperoning the dance to check on the kids and relieve other chaperones for a break. Many parents danced with each other.

Anthony took that moment to cozy up to her. He gestured to the dance floor. "I seem to have lost my dance partner. Would you care to dance with me?"

"As long as your *date* won't mind," she teased.

He gathered her into his arms, his hand pressed low on her back. With his strong heart beating against her, she luxuriated in the intimacy and comforting touch of how it felt to be held close in a man's arms. A place she hadn't been in such a very long time. She missed this—the warmth, the closeness.

Through her lashes, she glimpsed his eyes. Anthony was a gorgeous man.

He held her gaze and smiled.

What was he thinking?

His warm breath brushed her cheek, and he tightened his hold. Breathing in his woodsy scent, she melted against him, dropping her head against his chest. There was an emotional pull toward him which surprised her and left her questioning herself, as if she was betraying Dex.

Was it too soon?

She'd shied away from dating since her husband died. Even though this wasn't technically a date, her attraction to Anthony made her nervous. What would Dex think of her being held in another man's arms? Her mind ached from overthinking the situation. The idea of intimacy with another man was maddening.

Celine hadn't thought she'd feel anything like this again. Was it wrong to enjoy dancing in the arms of a man other than her husband? She didn't know how long he held her. All she knew was she never wanted him to let go.

Awash with emotions and trepidation, she took a step back when the song ended their dance.

It didn't take more than one dance for Anthony to see how the woman in his arms was affecting him. When Celine smiled at him, she rendered Anthony powerless to think of anyone else but her. At times, he had to remember to breathe.

Was this the beginning of something he never imagined? Something he welcomed and was ready to embrace? He'd yet to meet a woman he wanted to come home to.

Until now.

The moment he held her soft body in his arms, he knew he never wanted to give up the dark-haired beauty who took his breath away. And when the dance ended, he couldn't bear to let her go.

Bridget cleared her throat.

Anthony turned toward his sister and caught the amusement covering her face. He looked down at his fly, wondering if he'd forgotten to pull up the zipper.

"Hey, big brother. You should watch where you stand," she said with a sly grin covering her face.

He turned toward Celine standing next to him. "What's she talking about? Are you contagious with something I should know about?"

Celine and Bridget burst out laughing.

"You're standing under the mistletoe," Bridget pointed out.

Anthony glanced up. A large sprig of greenery hung above him. He gave a nod of his head, amused. "So I am." He looked from Bridget to Celine with a crooked grin. "I'm definitely not kissing my sister."

Celine's eyes twinkled.

He paused a beat, as if waiting for her approval. Anticipation surged through him.

She looked up at Anthony with the prettiest eyes, pulling him in, caressing his heart, shattering his resolve. He'd take that as a yes. His response was a smile that could melt a glacier. Pink tinged her cheeks as she smiled back, then her lips parted in a way that made him wish they were anywhere else other than inside a school surrounded by kids.

But he didn't move. He stared at her lips for a long moment, his brain battling with his body. Once he kissed her, it wouldn't be enough. He'd already fallen for her.

Hard.

She sent him a cheeky little grin. "Are you going to kiss me?"

His eyes glittered in response, and he leaned over her and said softly, "Oh, I'm definitely kissing you." Wrapping an arm around her waist and pulling her close, her warm body melted into his. He lost himself in the depth of her deep blue eyes as the seconds stretched on. With his other hand cupping her cheek, feeling the warmth of her skin beneath his fingertips, his lips touched hers. Soft, warm, pure heaven. She tasted like peppermint, the sweetness of her breath mingling with his own.

His groin tightened as he reveled in the taste of her. It took all his willpower to fight the urge to pull her even closer, trail his mouth to the hollow of her throat, and feel her pulse beneath his lips.

"Damn, Anthony. Let the woman breathe," Bridget reminded him.

The moment went on longer than expected, but not nearly long enough for him. He felt instantly guilty, but damn, she did it for him.

Sliding his hand down her lower back, he broke the kiss and let her go. The two of them lingered for an awkward moment. Her face flushed with a sweet pink blush. He hoped he hadn't overstepped until he glimpsed the look in her eyes and the smile hovering at the corners of her mouth.

"Merry Christmas, Celine," he said with a heart-stopping smile. Desperately wanting to pull her back into his arms and explore the simmering passion that had been building between them, he was thankful there were children in the room. Otherwise, the temptation to kiss her again would have been too strong to resist.

He'd have to thank his sister later for putting that holiday weed in the gymnasium. Best thing she'd ever done for him. Anthony hadn't enjoyed himself so much in years.

He met his sister's eyes and caught the twinkle, as if she'd intentionally placed the mistletoe there and assumed the role of matchmaker.

Savannah and her friends ran up to them. "Mommy, you're

not supposed to be here. My turn to dance with Anthony."

"I know when I'm not welcome," Celine said with a laugh and returned to the lounge with the other mothers.

Bridget followed, dropped into the chair beside her, and stretched out her legs in front of her. "I'm beat."

"You must be. Did you have time to go home for a few hours before the dance started?"

"I wish. Several of us teachers had to decorate for tonight."

"Tomorrow you can relax and enjoy your day off."

Bridget took a long drink of her water. "If only. Tomorrow I have to finish my Christmas shopping. Time is running out. Then there's Christmas at my brother Rob's house and I'm helping him cook. And I have to squeeze in time to go to my father's ranch in Saratoga to pick vegetables."

"He grows them in winter?"

"Dad has an enormous greenhouse. His tomatoes are great for canning. There's nothing like marinara sauce or chili made with homegrown tomatoes."

"I'm getting hungry thinking about chili," Celine said.

"Anthony likes chili. You should make a pot and invite him over."

Celine lifted an eyebrow. "Stop trying to fix me up."

Bridget grinned. "Then there's all the zucchini to make zucchini bread."

"I'd love a zucchini if there are any extra."

"I'll bring you back several. He also likes zucchini bread."

Celine's eyebrows rose.

Then a thought occurred to Bridget. "Would you and Savannah like to go with me? It won't be until after Christmas. She'd get a kick out of all the chickens and horses Dad has. I may stay overnight, fyi."

"I'd love to go, but there's a contractor I'm meeting at the house for an inspection once I get back from our trip."

"Would you let Savannah go with me? I know she's still

young, and I'll understand if you say no."

"I trust you. And Savannah loves you. How about if I let her decide?" Celine posed, and then had another thought. "I'm curious about something. Tell me if I'm being too nosey. Why are we always talking about me and how I should start dating? How come you're not dating anyone? What happened to the pilot?"

Bridget threw her head back and closed her eyes. "He broke my heart. I've sworn off men for the foreseeable future."

"I am so sorry for asking."

"It wasn't me. It was him, or so he said."

"His loss." Celine leaned back in her chair, shaking her head. "Men…"

"Yeah, getting dumped is not something to brag about."

Once the dance ended, Anthony returned Savannah to the lounge where most all the mothers filled the chairs, chatting and catching up on gossip. Celine sat sipping coffee, her brown hair pulled back into a messy bun.

Savannah ran up to her mother, giggling with a broad smile. "Mommy! Mommy! The dance was so much fun!"

Celine hugged her daughter before sneaking a peek at Anthony. His own smile broadened when she caught his eye.

"Savannah, I need to ask you something," Bridget said. "Later in the week, I'm going to my father's ranch to feed the horses and pick vegetables from his garden. It's an overnight trip. I'd love to have company if you'd like to go with me."

Savannah's face brightened as she looked at her mother. "Can I, Mommy? I'll have so much fun! Please?"

"I won't be able to go," Celine told her. "Will you be okay with that? Going with Bridget?"

"I'm a big girl. We'll have fun," Savannah replied.

Celine turned toward Bridget and saw her grin. "Okay, as long as you brush your teeth at night and don't stay up too late. And be good for Miss Callahan."

Savannah jumped up and down before engulfing her mother in an enormous hug. "Thank you!"

"Let's go grab a few snacks for our road trip." Bridget took Savannah's hand, and they went off to the snack table.

Which left Celine alone with Anthony. He sat down in the chair next to her and caught her gaze. "I apologize if I overstepped earlier."

"You didn't." Her cheeks grew warm just thinking about the kiss. "It's just…no one has kissed me like that in such a long time."

He hadn't planned it, but that kiss cemented his attraction to her. The more time he spent with her, the more he liked her. Celine's sweet demeanor was doing a number on him. That she was a smart, beautiful woman added to her allure. Bridget sang her praises as a great friend and dedicated mother, and much of that he had seen for himself.

"You must let me treat you to lunch, to thank you for taking Savannah. How about tomorrow?" Celine asked him.

"I have an obligation at my father's company in the early afternoon. How does dinner sound instead?" he countered.

"I'm not sure I can get a sitter on short notice with all the Christmas parties going on. Would you like to come to my place for dinner?"

"I'd love to."

Savannah returned with a handful of snacks. "Mommy, I'm tired."

"I'll walk you home." Anthony held his arms out to Savannah. "Your feet must be tired from all that dancing. I'll carry you."

When Anthony picked her up, she dropped her head on his shoulder and yawned. She kept him warm the entire way home and was sound asleep by the time they reached the cottage.

"She's asleep. Would you like me to put her on her bed?"

Celine unlocked the door and held it open. "Follow me." She led the way to the small bedroom. Savannah never stirred as Anthony gently laid her on her bed. Celine removed her shoes and covered her with a blanket, and they quietly left the room.

"Thank you, Anthony. For everything. Savannah had a wonderful time thanks to you," Celine said at the front door.

"It was my pleasure." Not wanting to leave, but knowing he should, his gaze lingered over her for a long moment.

What the hell.

"Now that we don't have an audience or any pressure from the mistletoe, this kiss is because I want to." He stared down at her and the heat rose in her cheeks. His fingers curled around the back of her neck and he brought his mouth down to hers, kissing her slowly and tenderly. Her soft lips yielded the way he'd known they would.

He broke the kiss and smiled. "I look forward to dinner tomorrow night."

She touched her fingers to her lips as she watched him walk out the door. Her pulse hadn't slowed and her lips still tingled. She breathed in deeply. Anthony's masculine scent, mixed with the spicy scent of his cologne, still lingered around her.

His kiss had rekindled the embers he'd left burning from the mistletoe kiss. At the school, she'd gotten caught up in the moment and let herself enjoy the time-honored tradition of a man kissing her under the mistletoe. How his lips felt against hers this time let her know he wanted to kiss her. He desired her. This kiss proved as much and had suddenly changed things between them.

Anthony became a man she wanted to get to know better.

And now she couldn't stop thinking about him.

16

Celine woke to the sound of soft breathing. When she lowered her hand to her side, her fingers brushed over the soft fur. Instantaneously, the sounds of purring began.

"Good morning, Tucker. Why are you in here with me and not with Savannah?"

Tucker stretched and stood up, brushing her body against hers.

"You're probably hungry. Okay, girl, let's find you some food." Celine sat up and before she could get out of bed, Savannah ran into her bedroom and went straight to her cat.

"There you are, Tucker." Savannah picked up her cat and carried her from the room.

Celine raked her fingers through her hair and went into the kitchen to feed them both.

"Mommy! Tucker got out!" Savannah yelled out.

"How did she get outside?"

"I opened the door to look at the Christmas decorations."

Celine couldn't find her robe and didn't have time to look for it. The fog cast the dim morning in gray. It would be easy for Tucker to hide. She had to find her. She was an indoor cat and would never survive outside.

Stepping from the cottage, she scanned the yard. Celine

saw the movement of leaves rustling under a shrub. She ran barefoot to it and located the cat. Just as she bent over and scooped her up, she heard *his* voice.

"Need any help?" Anthony asked in a husky tone.

Celine immediately glanced up to see Anthony watching her, his gaze moving slowly up and down her body. Their eyes locked, and she noted an amused grin. He stood behind her wearing a white T-shirt that hugged his chiseled chest against the thin fabric, low slung sweatpants under an open, fluffy gray robe, and black slippers.

It was then she realized she wasn't wearing much. All she had on was a pair of boxer shorts and a skimpy tank top, leaving nothing to the imagination. A shiver ran through her, hoping he mentioned nothing about her attire. Her face reddened, her cheeks blazing hot, and she stumbled over her words. "Retrieving a runner."

She stood up, holding the tabby. Anthony reached out and scratched under its chin. As if on cue, the tabby began to purr. "She likes you. The shelter told us she normally doesn't like men."

"Animals like me. I had a menagerie while growing up."

She blinked and couldn't help noticing the deep blue of his eyes, like a smokey lapis or a deep blue sea. Eyes she could easily get lost in. They weren't friendly or neighborly, either. They were fire and heat, and every part of her became engulfed in flames at the thought of his body pressed against hers. Sexual tension simmered between them. An attraction lit by a spark threatening to grow into a wildfire.

He moved forward toward her, closing the distance between them, his male sensuality filling the space. His gaze remained heated as it flickered over her like a storm brewing, and her body answered with feelings she tried to deny.

She could deny it all she wanted, but it was there. An urge to run her fingers through his dark locks and feel how soft his hair felt. She forced herself to take a step back, take a breath, keep a clear head, and push those thoughts away.

Celine had never felt so conflicted in her life. She needed to be smart about men, not blinded by lust. She wasn't looking to attract him, and it was crazy to feel being carried away by him so quickly.

She'd only known him for a short time, but it felt like she'd known him her entire life. Nothing she told herself could deny the intense pull like a magnet and the lingering allure she felt when he was around her. The man awakened urges deep within her, as if seeing the sun for the first time in months.

And my God, he was a gorgeous man. She had an inkling that her self-imposed hiatus from dating was about to end.

Anthony lowered his gaze, taking in the beautiful woman in front of him. Her eyes shimmered like the night sky. With her tousled hair as if she had just woke up, his thoughts strayed and he couldn't help but wonder if she looked that way after sex?

Peeking out of the skimpy tank and snug boxers was a fit body. A body which made his own come alive with a primal reaction. He had to look away, doing his best to shut that down.

This woman had turned his life upside down in a flash. After his wife died, he never thought he'd ever feel serious about a woman again. Not until Celine walked into his world had he craved more. He wanted Celine for keeps.

Now, thinking over the odd sense of circumstances with Savannah that had brought Celine into his life, and the way the woman made his pulse race, he thought that fate and destiny were indeed a possibility. Temptation stood in front of him and having her yards away from his house had him second guessing himself if this was such a good idea having her so close. But the woman and her daughter tugged at his heartstrings, and under the circumstances, opening up his cottage to them was the right thing to do.

He wanted to see more of this sweet, sexy woman. Have her fill his days and nights, see her smile, laugh with him. And not only that, but kiss her, protect her, love her. Do things a man does with a woman that he shouldn't be contemplating.

He was playing with fire.

He closed the gap and stepped closer.

The front door of the cottage opened, and Savannah stepped out. "Mommy, did you find Tucker?"

"She's right here," Celine replied.

Anthony watched as a smile spread across Savannah's face. She ran up to her mother to take the cat from her.

"Good morning, Savannah," Anthony greeted her.

Savannah gave him a sweet smile as she held tight to her cat. "Mommy's going to make cinnamon rolls this morning. Do you like cinnamon rolls?"

"My favorite breakfast."

Savannah looked at her mother. "Mommy, can Anthony stay for breakfast?"

Anthony gave Celine a smile that lit up his striking blue eyes, which were filled with amusement.

"Of course he can stay." She looked at Anthony, then recalled his meeting. "But I think he already has plans."

"I'm free for an hour. I'll go inside and change."

"Don't change," Savannah insisted. "We can have a pajama party breakfast!"

"You heard what the boss said," Celine said with a grin. "Come in. I'll start the coffee."

After grabbing a bathrobe from her closet, Celine put the cinnamon rolls into the oven.

Anthony helped himself to the coffee and came up beside her and handed her a steaming cup.

"Thank you."

"I wasn't sure if you liked cream and sugar," he said.

"A little of both. I've got it."

They sat down at the table and listened to Savannah chatter away about her Christmas garden. Her face glowed brightly as she showed Anthony the letters Teddy the elf had left for her. Celine noted the genuine interest he took in her daughter.

The oven timer went off, and she pulled the rolls from the oven. His gaze strayed to her beautiful face as Savannah helped her ice the cinnamon rolls while they talked about their holiday plans. There was something special about her just by watching her interact with her daughter.

Savannah brought him a plate of cinnamon rolls. She sat down beside him while they ate.

"We're leaving for Connecticut tomorrow. It's a quick trip. We'll only be gone for a few days," Celine said.

"What about your cat?" he asked.

"Bridget has promised to look in on Tucker while we're away."

"Mommy, I need to let Teddy know to watch over my garden while we're gone. I wrote him a note. Can we leave it for him today?" Savannah said.

"Of course we can."

"You must have a million things to do before your trip. I'll see you later for dinner," Anthony said, standing.

He wanted to steal a quick kiss, but with Savannah there, it didn't feel right. Celine looked up and pressed her lips together, and he couldn't help but imagine them on his mouth. Or other places.

17

After his meeting, Anthony stopped by Savannah's garden. He left a purple magnet of a unicorn he'd picked up at a little trinket store after leaving his meeting. He found a note left in the garden for *Teddy* and picked it up. A smile crossed his face as he read it.

Dear Teddy,

Thank you so much for the stickers. They are so nice. Thank you for living in the tree above our Christmas garden. Can you keep a lookout over our garden for the next few days? I'm going to visit my grandma and grandpa for Christmas. I'll be home in a few days.

Love, Savannah

What he wasn't expecting as he parked his truck in the driveway was seeing Matt Franklin leaving the cottage.

What the hell was he doing there?

There was only one reason. Celine.

He was confident she hadn't a clue to the man's character. Franklin was nothing but a predator, and Celine deserved to know the truth.

He crossed the yard straight to the cottage and knocked on the door.

"Anthony. You're a few hours early," Celine said, surprise clear on her face.

"I saw Franklin leave as I got home."

"He brought by a Christmas gift for Savannah."

"Be careful around him."

She stared at him, perplexed.

"There are some things about him you may not be aware of."

Her smile died as she studied his expression. "What are you talking about?"

He scrubbed a hand across his face. "It's none of my business who you socialize with, but I've seen the way he treats women."

"Seriously?"

"Just hear me out. Please."

She planted her hands on her hips and stared at him. "Before you say anything else, I know all about Matt. He and Dex were partners for years, so I have firsthand knowledge of how Matt can juggle three or four women at once. What did you think? That I would go out with him?"

His head jerked up. "I don't know what I thought. I just don't want to see you get hurt."

"There's nothing between us like that. Matt and I are friends, nothing more. And there never will be anything else."

He grimaced, his surprise clear. "He has a dark side you may not be aware of. I've seen it firsthand."

"I understand men like to think of themselves as cavemen and need to protect us women, but I'm a grown woman and can take care of myself without interference."

"Now you sound like my sister."

"I can handle Matt." She reached out and touched his arm. "Although I appreciate you looking out for me."

"I apologize for overreacting."

"You're forgiven."

The door swung all the way open, and they both turned to see Savannah's smiling face. He took the opportunity to step back and make his retreat. "So, dinner's still on?"

Her expression told him all he needed to know. "I'm looking forward to it."

When he returned for dinner, Celine had pulled her hair into a ponytail. She wore a soft, cream-colored sweater over a pair of snug jeans. Anthony tried not to notice how they hugged her curves.

But his body noticed.

"Dinner smells delicious, but you have to stop feeding me. I'm afraid I'll get pudgy from all the comfort food and sweets," he half-heartedly complained.

Celine sent him an amused look. "No one is forcing you to eat my cooking."

"It's hard to say no when it's made with such love by an amazing woman I'm having a hard time staying away from."

The corners of her mouth turned up and her cheeks turned pink at Anthony's words. "I'm more ordinary than amazing."

"Not in my book." He watched her and Savannah cooking in his cottage kitchen, looking right at home. The space felt warm and cozy. More than it ever had for him when he lived in it while he had his house painted.

After dinner, Anthony helped Celine with dishes while Savannah went to her bedroom to put on her pajamas.

"It's nice to have someone to do dishes with. Savannah loves to cook, but she hasn't yet grasped the art of completely rinsing the suds off the plates before putting them into the cabinet," she said, handing him a plate to dry and put away.

"She's still young."

"I have some wine. Would you like some?"

"Only if you'll join me."

"I'll get the glasses if you can get a bottle from the wine rack."

They moved at the same time and bumped into each other. He reached out to steady her, his hand gripping her arm. She looked up at him, her eyes focused on his as if she was also aware of the sexual energy building between them. For one long moment, their gazes held, and then his eyes slid down to her mouth.

Slightly parted.

Anthony swallowed.

Hard.

Savannah came into the kitchen carrying a blanket and her favorite stuffed animal. "Mommy, I'm tired. Can me and Tucker go to bed and read a book?" A long playdate had exhausted her.

"Of course you can. I'll never say no to you for wanting to read. Say goodnight to Anthony first."

The little girl with the sweet smile wrapped her arms around him and looked up at him with sleepy eyes. "Goodnight, Anthony."

"Goodnight, Savannah. Sweet dreams."

When Celine returned to the living room after tucking her daughter into bed, Anthony stood at the front window, looking out. "Anthony…"

He turned to face her. All he could see were her midnight blue eyes staring at him. It was then he knew what he wanted.

Her.

A life with Celine.

Ever since he'd kissed her under the mistletoe, the urge to gather her in his arms was intense.

He stepped forward, closing the distance between them, and searched her face. "I want to spend more time with you, see where this goes." Taking her hand in his, he went on, "I have feelings for you, Celine, and they're growing much faster than you might be ready for."

With a lift of her chin, her eyes glimmered. "I'm attracted to you and I'm not sure what to do with my feelings. I'd like to get to know you better."

He could memorize every curve of her lips perfectly, just a breath away. "I don't want to rush you into anything you're not ready for." He wanted to kiss her. It was so tempting. "Would it be okay if I held you?" She said nothing as his gaze trailed over her lips. "Or even kissed you?"

They shared a moment as she absorbed his words, and with a shy nod of her head, he touched her. The moment his fingers grazed her cheek, she lifted her gaze to his. Her skin melted into his touch as his fingers lingered. Without thinking of anything but her, he brushed his lips over hers. Warm, soft lips reminded his body he was a man who wanted this woman.

Inhaling the scent of her left him craving more. Anthony deepened the kiss, his hand curling around her waist. She was soft and yielding. Holding her against him felt right. So damned right. His body responded in kind, turning hard as granite. He wanted her badly, imagining how it would feel to be caressing her body as he moved over her slowly in his bed.

He lifted his gaze to hers. In her eyes, he saw desire matching his own. The warmth of the moment lingered in the air, and the need to give in to his want became stronger. His hands fell on her hips, pulling her firmly against him, feeling the heat radiating between them. A low, involuntary groan escaped him.

"Anthony," she breathed out, her voice a mixture of emotions, before stepping back and averting her eyes.

"I'm sorry. What you do to me…" He had to slow down. She wasn't his yet to love.

She sat down on the sofa, and he joined her. "You surprised me. I wasn't expecting this...us, to be this intense, so...all consuming."

"I want you to be comfortable. Tell me if I'm moving too fast." He noticed a flicker of anxiety in her eyes. "We can make this work, however you like," he assured her.

After meeting his eyes for a long moment without words, she leaned over and brushed her lips lightly against his cheek. "All I ask is for you to be gentle with my heart."

Her vulnerability left him momentarily speechless, reminding him of how much she'd been through, and how much she meant to him. He drew her into his arms, gathering her close, and she went willingly, sinking into his comforting embrace. His arms remained gentle around her, soothing with a light touch.

"I've been alone for a long time. After my wife died, I felt numb for the longest time. You and Savannah have brought warmth and light back into my life when I needed it most. I'm ready for a relationship."

For an answer, she lifted a hand to his cheek. "I sometimes forget I'm not the only one who has lived with pain and needs love in their life."

As she ran her hand over his chest, settling into his arms, it seemed she needed him as much as he did her.

He had never known a sweetness like Celine. Stroking her hair, sliding his fingers through the silky strands, left his senses spinning. "Wanting you is only the beginning. We'll go slow, at your pace."

"I think I need you, too. This is new to me, and I'm not sure where to start."

He released the breath he didn't realize he'd been holding. "We might start with this." He slid his hand around her nape, pulling her closer. Inhaled her scent—vanilla, like everything sweet he had ever wanted. With her lips a breath away from his mouth, he kissed her, gently at first, slow dancing on her lips until her blood ignited and she ran her fingertips up his back, pulling him closer.

One kiss led to another and another. Anthony wrapped his arms around her body, bringing her into a possessive embrace. She fit in his arms as if he was born to hold her.

Celine closed her eyes as passion and hunger rippled between them. A soft sigh escaped her when his lips went from a slow roaming journey over her skin to searing a path over her neck, along her collarbone, devouring her with each kiss.

He ached to feel her closer. His hand lingered on her thigh, and with a mind of its own, it moved slowly upward, tracing a path up her leg. Then he stopped and drew his hand back, forcing himself to slow down.

"Mommy!" Savannah called out from her bedroom.

They jerked apart. Immediately, Celine pulled away, breathless. "I'll get her back to sleep."

He watched her go to her daughter and followed, standing outside the room, leaning against the doorjamb. As he watched her soothe her child and kiss her cheek, a need that went beyond anything he had ever felt for a woman filled him. He wanted to look at her beautiful face for the rest of his life.

Celine was meant to be his.

A small smile crossed his lips. Now was the time to make sure she knew it. He went back to the living room and waited for her.

Minutes later, Celine entered the room and found him standing in front of the fireplace. "She's asleep."

He was all too aware of her. The soft gait of her steps, the sound of her voice, her scent wafting around him. Shifting his attention from the blazing fire to the woman, agonizingly close, all he could think about was the taste of her lips. How it felt to hold her in his arms. The atmosphere felt heavy now, laden with want, desire. They couldn't tear their eyes from each other.

"Would you like some more wine?" she asked, moving to refill their glasses before sitting down on the sofa.

He moved beside her and brushed the hair away from her forehead. "I'm crazy about you. The only thing I want is the taste of your lips." Anthony leaned over and pressed his mouth against hers. The kiss was tender and yet filled with passion and longing. His arms went around her waist, drawing her to him, basking in the feel of her in his arms, and loving everything about her. An embrace filled with promise. Something he hadn't felt for a long time.

Anthony made her laugh, flirted endlessly, and when his touch lingered longer than necessary, she welcomed it, ached for it. He made her feel alive.

The moment his lips touched hers, she wanted more. Turning and pressing her lips to his mouth, as greedy for him as he was for her, fires ignited everywhere they touched. The heated kiss nearly stopped her heart as she wound her arms around his neck, sliding her hands through his hair.

Lost in the overwhelming need for each other, the air between them crackled like dry brush in a forest fire. His kiss devoured her, leaving her breathless and begging for more. Brushing his fingers along her cheek, replacing his lips on the same spot, left her whimpering, setting her body on fire like never before.

He slid his hands under her sweater, sliding up her back until he found her bra. In less than five seconds, he had unhooked the latch, leaving her unencumbered. Under her sweater, his hands kneaded her breasts, and she swallowed a groan. "Oh, God, that feels so good."

Anthony took pleasure in the sounds she made. He lifted her to straddle his lap, gripped her hips, holding her still, face-to-face. Their eyes connected, heat smoldering between them. The corners of his mouth curved upward before his warm lips brushed against her forehead.

Celine ran her hands across his muscled chest, savoring the warmth of his body against hers. "You feel amazing," she whispered, holding on to his shoulders.

Anthony brought his mouth to hers in a heated kiss. "Tell me you want me as much as I want you," he whispered against her lips.

She ran her hands through his thick dark hair, not wanting to think—just needing to touch, feel, surrender.

He lifted her chin, and his eyes held hers. "I want to love you." He didn't move and waited for her answer.

Her chest heaved up and down and the rumble of his deep voice drew her back to reality. "Anthony," she murmured huskily as his words and the carnal intent in his eyes brought everything back into sharp focus. This close, he flooded her mind and heart with sensations she did not know what to do with. In the midst of passion, she realized their friendship had blossomed into much more than a deep connection. She was in over her head the longer he kissed her, knowing where they were headed.

She closed her eyes and stilled.

What am I doing?

Shaken by emotions and the heat of the moment, Celine took in a sharp breath and pulled away. Although she couldn't deny she wanted him, she'd gotten lost in the spell of lust, and needed to step back and make sure she did nothing she'd regret later.

"We need to slow down."

He pulled away but didn't let go and never took his eyes off her. "I'll go as slow as you want."

"We can't do this. Not with Savannah in the other room."

He pressed his forehead against hers. Every cell in his body burned for her. "I think you might be right."

"It's more than that." She hesitated a long moment. "I'm not sure I'm ready for you."

"I understand." As if reading her mind, he said, "You still love him."

Celine said nothing for a long time, and then looked into his eyes, fighting back tears. "I don't mean to hurt you. It's just...it feels as if I'm cheating on him."

"This might be too soon for you. It's all right to feel that way."

What was happening between them was intense. Her hands shook. She wasn't sure what to do with the heated, humming sensation rushing through her. Anthony had an intense sexual energy she wasn't ready for.

He brushed the hair back from her eyes. "I'm not asking you to forget about him. Never would I do that. Until you're ready, I'll wait. I'm not going anywhere. The only thing I ask is for you to make a space inside your heart for me."

He drew her closer. "I don't want you to think of him when we make love. When it happens, the only man I want you thinking about is me. I want you to see *me* in your pretty eyes when I make you mine."

18

There was no relaxing around the fire in the hearth once Celine and Savannah reached her mother's home. Celine opened the door, and Christmas music, laughter, and several voices greeted them.

Her mother, Marie, had plans for the afternoon they arrived. She loved to host parties and organized a gathering of extended family and friends. Spread out over her dining room table were hors d'oeuvres, finger foods, sweets, and all the eggnog and spiced rum one could want.

Cousins Celine hadn't seen in years stopped by before the group left for her mother's first group activity. They attended the downtown Christmas tree lighting event, a yearly tradition. Her family loved the holiday season and never missed the lighting ceremony of the town's historic tree.

It couldn't have been a more beautiful evening. The snow had stopped falling. The city blocked off the streets for pedestrians only, and it appeared the entire town had shown up.

The aroma of hot apple cider wafted through the air. Neighbors and friends milled about, chatting and laughing. Booths selling mistletoe, fresh cherry pies, and locally designed ornaments dotted the square. High schoolers handed out cups of steaming hot chocolate to everyone trying to stay warm. Christmas carolers wandered about through the downtown plaza singing carols and spreading good cheer.

Celine saw couples holding hands and stop under the many sprigs of mistletoe left hanging under the overhangs of shops. The couples would linger for a kiss and giggle before moving on hand in hand. Celine missed that. The simple comforting pleasure of holding hands with a man. The thought reminded her of the many times she and Dex had strolled the same streets with his warm hand curled around hers, holding tight.

She looked down at her daughter and saw his same eyes on her face, smiling back at her. She gave her a quick hug, and they moved on through the streets with their fingers entwined.

Celine loved sharing with Savannah a taste of her own childhood experience. Savannah's eyes widened once she stood in front of the massive spruce tree decorated with sparkling garland, shining ornaments, and big, beautiful red bows. The crowd continued the longstanding tradition and sang Jingle Bells, Silent Night, and other songs everyone knew by heart.

Only when Santa Claus arrived on his sleigh pulled by real live reindeer, did the festivities heartily begin. Jolly St. Nick took his place of honor and lit the small town's tree, holding thousands of twinkling lights of every color, brilliant and glowing bright. Children gasped in delight and an encore of singing ensued.

Once the ceremony had concluded, they went back to her mother's house, exhausted. Savannah fell asleep as soon as her head touched the pillow.

The next day was Christmas Eve. Celine took Savannah to see Dex's family. For an instant, Celine saw raw grief reflected in her mother-in-law's eyes as she hugged Savannah. As she held her granddaughter tight, her expression quickly turned to joy.

Linda released Savannah and moved to give Celine a heartfelt hug. "I've missed you both so much. How are you?"

"Other than the fire I told you about, we're doing well."

A roaring fire in the fireplace kept them warm as they opened gifts, drank eggnog, and caught up on each other's lives. Savannah regaled them with tales about Teddy the elf, who lived in the tree where her garden was located, and all the kind letters he had sent to her.

After lunch, Dex's father took Savannah on a walk around the block with his dog. Linda made a pot of tea and they sat down in the kitchen for a long chat.

"So how are you? Really?" Linda asked, now that they were alone.

"Grief counseling has helped me. I no longer cry every day."

"It's all right to cry, even every day if you want to."

"Sometimes it's hard not to. I'm doing my best to raise Savannah with a sense of normalcy."

"She seems happy."

"She has her moments of crying for her daddy."

Savannah had wonderful memories of her father, but being so young, she didn't understand the circumstances of how he had died. Celine would tell her when she was older.

Dex's parents understood what Celine felt—the devastation of Dex's death. He was their son and shared the same loss. Celine had always been close with Linda, and Linda was one of the few she could be honest with about the impact of Dex's death and how it had affected her and Savannah. Celine had lived with a deep sorrow for a long time after he passed, and it only now felt as if it were lifting some.

"I talk often with Savannah about Dex," Celine said. "Keeping his memory alive is important to me."

"It's important to all of us. But Dex would want us to be happy and not bury ourselves in our grief. Are you getting out and doing things for yourself?"

"Some." Celine considered for a moment. "No, not really. At times, I have an overwhelming feeling of being lost. Dex was my anchor."

"What you're feeling is normal. It's part of the grieving process. Be patient. You'll find your way."

"I'm not sure I ever will."

"Don't doubt yourself. You're still young and have so much life to live. Don't hide yourself away." Linda searched her eyes and what she saw there worried her. "I wanted to ask you…" she began cautiously, "Have you thought about dating again?"

"I'm not putting myself *out there*, if that's what you're asking."

She never mentioned Anthony. What they had was too new to even mention. And she had no clue if it would go anywhere beyond their friendship, the dinners they had, and the kisses they shared.

"It's okay to move forward. Your life is waiting for you. Dex would want you to be happy, to find love again."

Celine stared at Linda in disbelief. "I'm not sure I can do that. He was the love of my life. I loved Dex more than anyone."

"I know you did, sweetheart. You had a good life with Dex. He loved you more than life itself. But he's no longer alive." Linda reached out and covered Celine's hand with hers. "And you are. Be happy."

"I still love him."

"Oh, honey, you'll always love him. You have so much love inside your heart. But don't close yourself off to finding someone else to love. The best way to honor his memory is not to hide away, but to live. He'd want that for you."

Celine didn't know what to say. She'd managed to pick up the pieces and move forward for the sake of her daughter. But it was difficult letting go of Dex. She wasn't sure if she would ever love again.

"Just know, you have our blessing to find happiness again. If you meet another man who loves you as much as my son did, don't hesitate to love him back. And if the time comes for you to marry again, I don't want our phone calls to end. I hope you'll introduce us. You'll always be family, and we will always be there for you, no matter what."

Celine reached out and hugged Linda. "I love you so much."

"It means everything to his father and me to be a part of your life. We don't want it to change."

It meant so much to hear this sort of encouragement and support from her. Celine realized she'd never have a life again with Dex. He was her past. The best she could do was keep him alive in Savannah's heart and mind. But it wasn't enough to only have the memories. Savannah needed a strong male influence in her life going forward.

Anthony had made a positive impact on her daughter. And Savannah adored him.

Celine thought of Anthony then, and her heart felt heavy. A complicated mixture of emotions churned deep inside her. Celine often dismissed what she wanted for herself, taking a backseat to her daughter's needs. As time passed by, Celine yearned for a normal life full of friendship and love. And more recently, she'd felt a longing to be loved. But still, she hesitated.

I want to feel loved again, but I'm afraid of leaving Dex behind.

Then someone entered her life and began chipping away at the walls she'd built up.

Anthony. He'd changed her.

He wanted a relationship. He'd made that clear. Anthony had already told her how he felt about her and he was willing to give her time until she was ready to give herself fully.

She searched her heart to find the answer to what *she* wanted. It would be so easy to fall in love with him.

Could Anthony be the man she needed in her life?

After going back to her parent's home and getting Savannah tucked into bed, Celine made her way to her own room. Her childhood bedroom. The same room she'd share with Dex whenever they came home to visit.

The house was still, and she lay awake for a long time. Memories of Dex filled her mind and warmed her heart. He'd be so proud of Savannah.

Losing him taught her about how much she wanted to live. How she needed to find joy in her own life, not only for their daughter, but for herself. Linda's words filtered through her mind. Could she open her heart to find love again?

It scared the hell out of her.

Every time she closed her eyes, Dex was there. She longed to hear him tell her he loved her and to have just one more hug from him. She drifted off to sleep, remembering all the wonderful moments they had together. How much love they shared.

Oh, Dex, how do I move on from you?

A few days later, Celine blinked open her eyes. She felt light and refreshed as the dream still whispered through her mind. And oddly, it wasn't so much that she had dreamt about him.

She felt Dex's presence in the room.

She pulled on her bathrobe and looked out the window. The morning sun warmed her face. A light snow had fallen overnight and was beginning to melt. A surge of warmth washed over her heart. Wrapping her arms around herself, she recalled the dream as a calmness filtered through her.

Dex held Savannah in his arms as he moved toward Celine. He leaned down and gently kissed his daughter on the cheek before placing her in Celine's arms.

"My love is always with you. Give our daughter the life she deserves. The life you both deserve to live."

She'd wanted to reach out and touch his face.

But he'd walked away.

Celine didn't realize she'd been crying as Savannah bounded into her room and wrapped her arms around Celine's legs. "Mommy, Grandma made me pancakes, so I'd have a good breakfast before our trip."

Celine's heart warmed at how her mother loved to spoil her granddaughter. "You have a wonderful grandmother. I hope you know how lucky you are."

Savannah looked up at her mother's face. "Are you okay, Mommy?"

"I'm more than okay, baby." She bent over her daughter and kissed her. "Let's go home."

19

After dropping off Savannah at a friend's house for a playdate, Celine went by her house to check on the remodel. The contractor told her he would need a few more days to finish the kitchen, but she could move back in sooner if she wished. The smoke removal company had done a great job with the mitigation work and the painters had repainted the walls of the first floor with fresh paint. They cleaned her furniture and moved it back in. It amazed her how quickly everything had come together. He told her things were slow during the holidays and he had many workers hungry to work. The job would finish well ahead of schedule.

She was fine with the timeline. They were warm and comfortable in the cottage, and there was no rush. A few days wouldn't make much difference.

That night, Celine and Savannah had plans with Anthony. He wanted to take them out for dinner and wander through Union Square to enjoy the holiday lights one last time before the city removed the decorations.

But before then, she thought she'd treat herself to breakfast and some quiet time she craved.

She shrugged on her jacket and headed for the cafe a few blocks away. A hidden gem frequented by neighborhood locals. Mamacita's served the best coffee and eggs benedict in the city.

She made a right turn on California Street and smiled the closer she got to the cafe. The aroma of fresh coffee wafted through the street. When she opened the door, the delicious scents of pastries and breakfast assaulted her senses, making her stomach growl.

A half dozen small tables topped with red and white checkered tablecloths covered the tables made of dark wood. A long counter with red stools that faced the kitchen ran to one side. Cozy, simple, inviting.

The place was busy. Ever since a TikTok influencer made a video raving about the delicious coffee they served, the video went viral and the crowds had picked up considerably.

They seated her, and when the server offered her a menu, she declined. Celine didn't need to view a menu. This morning called for eggs benedict. It was *that* kind of morning.

"Celine! What are you doing here?"

She looked up and noticed Bridget enter the cafe and make her way straight to her table. "Savannah has a playdate, so I'm enjoying some mommy time with *my friend* here." She held up her cup of coffee. "Caffeine is a necessity when you have a six-year-old."

"I need a pick-me-up after finishing up report cards. You should get Savannah's in the mail in a few days."

"Should I be worried?"

"Hardly. She's perfect."

"That's a relief."

Bridget grinned. "Be proud. She's one of my best students in class."

The server stopped at the table with a steaming pot. "Ready for a refill?"

Bridget turned her cup over. The server filled it and freshened up Celine's cup after she held up her cup and thanked her with a friendly smile.

Celine added some cream and sugar to her coffee, stirring it leisurely before taking a long sip.

Bridget noted her friend's quietness and leaned forward. "What has you so deep in thought?"

She forced a casual shrug. "Nothing. Enjoying my child free moment."

A fire engine raced through the street with its lights flashing and siren blaring. Celine craned her neck to look out the window.

"I see…"

Heat rushed to Celine's face.

"Looks more like you are thinking about a certain firefighter?"

Celine reached for her cup again and took a huge sip.

Why does it feel so hot in here?

"So, what's going on between you and my brother?"

Celine couldn't hide her smile, and wasn't sure she wanted to answer her friend's question.

But when Bridget raised an eyebrow, she coughed on the hot liquid.

"I've seen the way he looks at you. My brother has a serious thing for you," Bridget said. "So my question is, what are you going to do about it?"

Turning her gaze out the window, Celine thought about her question for a few moments before giving Bridget her full attention. "We have a date tonight. Anthony is taking me and Savannah out for dinner."

"Sounds like fun. But next date, plan a sleepover for Savannah with one of her friends," Bridget quipped.

Celine turned three shades of red. "What?"

"You heard me. I didn't stutter."

The city was still brimming with Christmas decorations and sparkling lights, keeping the festive holiday mood alive. Tonight, the streetlights remained decorated with green garland outlined with small twinkling lights.

Anthony took Celine and Savannah downtown to a child-friendly restaurant for an early dinner and gelato. He sat across from Celine and couldn't stop looking at her. "This is nice, but our date tomorrow is something I'm looking forward to."

"So am I, although you're being secretive about where we're going," she said, inclining her head.

He tore his gaze away from her hair, falling around her shoulders and his thoughts about running his fingers through it. "It's a surprise."

"I need to know what to wear. Do I need a ballgown or jeans for a rib joint?" she teased, her blue eyes sparkling.

"No ballgown, no jeans. Somewhere in between will be fine." A childless date he looked forward to the following evening.

After they finished their gelato, they strolled through Union Square, where an enormous decorated Christmas tree sparkled with thousands of lights in the middle of the square. Scattered throughout the park were booths selling candles, arts and crafts, wooden cable car trinkets, and other tourist goodies.

They stopped at a flower vendor, and Anthony picked out a beautiful bouquet of roses mixed with baby's breath for Celine. When he handed her the flowers, she gave him a smile that stole his heart.

They spent the next hour meandering through the shops or window shopping and admiring the holiday displays in store windows. Anthony generally avoided the downtown during the holidays. It brought back too many painful memories he'd rather not think about. But seeing the joy and wonder alive in Savannah's eyes gave him a new perspective. He enjoyed looking at Christmas through a child's eyes.

Savannah took Anthony's hand as they made their way toward the cable car line. She looked up at him, and the smile on her face warmed his heart. He'd met his match in the little girl and she had him totally wrapped around her finger.

On the way home, Savannah pulled his hand toward her magical garden. She'd reconstructed it since the fire so everyone could continue to enjoy it. A few people with smiles on their faces gathered around the garden, enjoying the holiday goodwill the garden provided.

"This has been a fun evening," Celine said as they made their way into the cottage. Savannah immediately ran to see her cat. "Savannah loved the cable car ride."

"I had fun hanging out with her."

Celine leaned in close so only Anthony could hear her. "Your *alter ego* has changed her. She needed *him* so desperately at a difficult time in her life. I want you to know you've made a positive impact on her. When Dex died, she retreated into herself, feeling lost. Teddy made her feel special and loved. Her self-confidence and shyness have improved. Since Teddy came into her life, her creativity has skyrocketed and her kindness towards others has come back full force, like the little girl she used to be."

"I'm happy to hear that."

"She's saved all the notes Teddy has written in a box where she holds all of her most precious treasures."

"She's a special little girl."

Celine appreciated how fortunate she was to have a daughter like Savannah. A cheerful, thoughtful child who placed the needs of her friends and even her mother before her own.

"And if it wasn't for her and her garden, I might never have met you," he added.

Celine's cheeks flushed. "Thank you for dinner. And for the flowers. They're beautiful."

They stood looking at each other for a long moment.

"I'm going to kiss you."

The way she smiled told him she had no objection. He leaned forward and kissed her softly on the lips. She slid her arms around his neck and he loved the taste of her, wanting more when she opened her mouth and his tongue pressed against hers. But before the fire could ignite any further, he pulled back and broke the heated kiss. They stared at each other, hearts pounding.

And then Anthony smiled. "I will see you tomorrow for our date."

At the door, she watched him leave. He seemed too good to be true. She didn't know where their relationship was headed, but all her doubts about dating him disappeared, leaving her happy she had met him and given him a chance.

20

Celine and Savannah spent the morning rushing through the house, packing a bag, and gathering a few toys and snacks for Savannah's overnight road trip with Bridget. They'd both overslept and were now moving through the house at lightning speed, trying to get ready before Bridget arrived.

When Bridget stepped through the door, she handed Celine an extra large mocha latte from the coffeeshop down the street.

"You are a lifesaver. I haven't had a drop of coffee yet this morning," Celine admitted.

"Up all night dreaming about my brother?" Bridget teased.

Celine blushed, not ready to admit to her friend or anyone —even herself—that she had strong feelings for him and was ready to embrace them.

Bridget raised an eyebrow. "He really likes you. I'd say he's falling hard for you like I've never seen before."

Celine enjoyed spending time with Anthony. They had become close friends. He made her laugh, feel alive, and special. And the way he kissed her…

"Looks to me like you have the hots for him, by the way you're blushing. Enjoy your childless time. And your date tonight."

Her face heated even more. "He told you?"

"Ha! He won't tell me anything. It's my job as his sister to pry it out of him."

After Celine's talk with her former mother-in-law, she'd given immense thought about moving forward with Anthony. His kindness toward a little girl's Christmas wish and her daughter's bright outlook on life had made Celine take a new look at her own life. She'd been through a lot.

She realized she'd always love Dex, but it was okay to move forward to live a full life. And if she was lucky enough, perhaps find love again. She wanted more out of life and was tired of being alone.

"Anthony is the first man I've gone out with since Dex."

"And?" Bridget prodded.

"He's a great guy."

"Told you."

"Of course you'd say that. He's your brother."

Bridget grinned. "I was just thinking, if you keep moving forward with this love tango, we may become sisters."

Celine's breath caught in her chest at the thought. "It's a little soon for that."

"I've seen the way you look at him. And how could I miss that kiss under the mistletoe?" Bridget noted Celine's blush. "You're falling for my brother, aren't you?"

Anthony had been upfront about his desire for a relationship. She liked him. If she was honest, she liked him much more than she cared to admit, but danced around her feelings for him. She was afraid to give him her heart. Was she ready for something so serious?

A smile crept across her lips. She could see everything clearly. It would be nice to see what a relationship with him would be like.

"Take this piece of advice from me. Lower the wall you have up. You can't hide from life. Don't be afraid to move on.

You and Anthony are lucky enough to find each other. Have the courage to follow your heart to wherever it leads you."

It was crazy. Dangerous even. Celine couldn't deny the attraction. The way he gave her butterflies just being near him. Even now, goose bumps peppered her skin just thinking about him. She took in a deep, steady breath.

She wanted him.

Maybe now it was time to let Anthony know how she felt.

"We're going to get out of your hair so you can nap before your date. I'm sure you won't get much sleep tonight."

Celine's mouth fell open.

Bridget sent her a sly grin and a wink. "Have fun."

Celine had a hard time choosing what to wear. Anthony had said to wear something in between a ballgown and jeans. Huh. A dress would be appropriate for a dinner date. Since the weather was cool, it had to have some substance. She pushed aside the flirty sundresses with spaghetti straps and found a new dress in the back of her closet that she hadn't yet worn. A soft, dark gray sweater dress which molded to her figure and showed off her curves felt right for a date night. Pairing it with black books finished the look.

After finishing her makeup with a smokey eye, and styling her hair in soft curls, she added a dab of a soft pink lip gloss and gave herself a nod of approval.

When she opened the door, Anthony's eyes took her in and he let out a low whistle and smiled. "Hello, gorgeous." He wrapped an arm around the small of her back and pulled her in for a kiss that left no doubt about his feelings for her.

Anthony took Celine to dinner at a small Italian restaurant in North Beach. They had a quiet table in the dimly lit restaurant and just enough privacy to make them feel as if they were all alone. The owner stopped by their table briefly to say hello, and had a bottle of wine sent over. On the house. Anthony seemed to know everyone in the place.

"Are you a regular here?" Celine asked, her eyes taking in her handsome date with his square jaw and vivid blue eyes.

"Six months ago, my crew responded to a fire inside the kitchen. We saved the restaurant with minimal damage to the kitchen. Ever since, we're treated like rock stars whenever we dine here."

"It's good karma to reward a good deed."

"It was our job."

"Well, I, for one, thank you for a job well done. You saved my home as well."

"And you brought my crew pie and ice cream to say thanks. We appreciated it."

They settled into easy conversation. Celine told him about her trip home and how happy Savannah had been to see her grandparents.

He studied her as they ate. The way her face lit up when she talked about her little patients at the hospital warmed his heart. She smiled proudly when she told him of her conversation with Savannah, suggesting they volunteer regularly at the animal shelter.

There was a natural chemistry between them and they spent the next hour lost in conversation. They had a great time during dinner, enjoying each other's company while the world around them faded away.

His gaze trailed over her as she sipped her white wine. This woman sitting across from him had enriched his life in so many ways too numerous to count. Celine was beautiful, smart, and sweet, with a smile that stole his heart the moment they met. His eyes never left hers during their conversations about their jobs, family, and his alternate ego—Teddy.

"How long will Savannah keep her garden in place?" he asked.

"I suggested taking it down soon and donating any toys that were left to the homeless shelter. Bridget thought she could use the garden as a teaching lesson in her class."

"Great idea."

"Are you close with Bridget?" she asked.

"Very. Although not as close as Christian is. They're twins and that favorite brother role is reserved for him. What about you? It must be difficult living across the country from your siblings."

"Both of my brothers are career military men. It's hard not seeing them as often as I used to when they were stationed in the States. I miss them a great deal and worry about Savannah growing up without her uncles or grandparents close by. It's just us out here on our own."

"What about your parents? Are you close with them?"

"Very. I miss them."

"Have you ever thought about moving closer to home?"

"The thought has crossed my mind."

He leaned back in his chair. "What's keeping you here?"

"Have you ever lived in the snow?"

He shook his head.

"It's pretty to look at…until you have to shovel it."

Anthony laughed. "I see your point."

"Savannah and I FaceTime my parents every few days, so that connection with my parents is there for her."

"You don't get to have much *me time* when you're doing everything by yourself."

"Which is one reason why I said yes when Bridget offered to take Savannah to your father's ranch for an overnighter."

"I'll have to thank my sister for giving me a chance to have you all to myself for an evening." He planned to enjoy every moment of their time together.

After a meal of shrimp scampi and tiramisu for dessert, he paid the bill, insisting even after the owner said it was on the house.

Crisp, cool air greeted them when they stepped outside. He offered his arm, and Celine took it, sliding her arm through his. The warmth of his body kept her toasty as they ventured through the neighborhood, enjoying the bright lights of the city.

They stopped for a few minutes to listen to a street performer play a guitar. His arm tightened around her as they listened to the love song being played. Anthony tossed a few dollars into the man's donation can after he finished the song, took Celine's hand, and they walked for a few blocks until Coit Tower came into view.

His arm dropped around her shoulders when they stopped to appreciate the San Francisco landmark. A slender concrete column rising from the top of Telegraph Hill lit up with color lighting the sky. Moments of silence passed between them as they admired the tower named for Lillie Coit, a wealthy patron of the city's firefighters.

He looked down at her, and she reached out to cup his face with both hands. "Let's go home." He barely registered her intent before she leaned forward and kissed him.

Anthony took her hand as they made their way the few blocks to her door. She took her key from her purse and met his gaze. He didn't say a word as he took the key from her hand, unlocked the door, and held it open for her.

When she turned to him, the expression in his eyes and the small smile that lingered at the corners of his mouth made her catch her breath.

He stepped forward and stroked her cheek with the back of his hand. "I enjoyed having dinner with you. But more than that, I'm grateful to have you in my life. You've reminded my heart of the joy and beauty of living." His other hand came up to the other side of her face and he brushed his lips over hers, loving how they felt against his.

He opened his arms, and she leaned into him, resting her head on his chest, his powerful arms around her with the strength of his body pressed against her. Anthony took in the moment, the intimacy of holding her in his arms tugging at something deep inside his heart. Tonight, everything would change between them.

He loosened his embrace, and when she looked up at him, something glittered in her eyes, drawing him in, sending electricity throughout his body. He lowered his mouth, kissing her tenderly. His chest tightened almost painfully as he deepened the kiss, and she welcomed him into the warmth of her mouth. His tongue danced with hers, and she smiled into his kiss, her hands running over his shoulders and snaking around his neck.

He stoked the sparks that crackled between them, causing flames to flicker into a fire, alive and growing. Anthony lost his ability to think as need made every cell in his body come alive. Her fiery kiss and warm body pressed against him soon shifted into an unbearable longing to be together, skin to skin.

As if reading his mind, she pushed his jacket from his shoulders and wrapped her arms around him, exploring the muscles of his back beneath her fingertips. Her body responded by pressing tighter against him and a soft groan escaped him.

He was hard everywhere, aching to feel her bare skin against him. His voice dropped an octave. "If you're not ready for this, tell me."

Celine slid her fingers along his jaw. "I'm sure." There was no stopping now. She pressed her mouth against his and brought the heat of her body into his.

Curling her into his chest, crushing her against him, he kissed her deeper, and she melted into him. The warm taste of her seeped into his blood, and he savored the sweetness of the woman in his arms. "I want to love you."

She took in a slow breath, tilting her head back, gazed into those gorgeous eyes of his and smiled. "Then love me."

Registering the desire in her eyes, he held her chin, angling her lips to meet his. Bending his head, he captured her lips, and indulged himself at last. He explored the shape of her lips, teased them apart and slipped inside, kissing her for all he was worth.

She clung to his shoulders with his mouth trailing a path of searing heat down the tender line of her neck. Her hands flew to his shirt, unfastening buttons, pushing the shirt aside to reveal the body of a Greek God. Every inch of him was sculpted to perfection. Seeking the need to feel his skin beneath her fingertips, she ran her palms over his bare, muscled chest. "We have entirely too many clothes on."

He grinned. Her dress was next to go. He lifted it over her head, dropping it to the floor, feasting his eyes on the woman before him. "Beautiful."

Bending to whisper in her ear, his lips traveled to her neck, while his hands glided down her body. Relishing the feel of her against him, his lips moved down her throat, grazing her delicate collarbone, dropping lower to her breasts, his warm mouth devouring her like a man with an unrelenting thirst.

Eyes closed, her head fell back as heat burned between them. She rocked against his powerful body, spurring him on.

When his lips met hers, the fire in his blood ignited. He ached for her, desire coiling deep inside him, wanting all of her. Locking eyes for a half a second, her blue eyes drew him in. A deep, low rumble sounded at the back of his throat. He hoisted her up into his arms and carried her to the bedroom, falling to the bed in a tangle of limbs.

Anthony trailed his finger along her cheek as his eyes filled with tenderness met hers, letting the connection between them linger. All he was aware of was the wonderful sensations of the woman in his arms. His mouth found her lips, kissing her tenderly, taking his time, as if he had only this one precious moment in time.

She was liquid fire in his arms, her body responsive to his every touch. She moaned with pleasure as he continued to explore every inch of her.

Anthony groaned, questioning his control as a wild need threatened to undo him. He tightened his arms around her, scraping his lips against hers, the tension building inside him until he was aching. Anthony never wanted to stop loving this woman who had captured his heart.

A sweet sigh escaped her, bewitching him, driving him crazy in the best kind of way, and his kiss turned demanding, diving deeper with the force of his feelings.

He wanted her today, tomorrow, forever…

21

Celine noted the hunger in his gaze. She ignored any conscious thought to slow down, not give in to her body's needs, any practical thought that this was madness. Nor did she want to fight her emotions or resist any longer. She wanted to feel again, love, surrender. Her eyes drifted closed the moment Anthony's lips touched hers.

She could feel his heart and hers as they both beat wildly. Beginnings of a new life she had doubted she was ready for until now, and yearned to discover. Her fingertips gently skimmed his chest, drifting to his stomach. He inhaled sharply, as if he couldn't breathe.

Throwing caution aside, she deepened the kiss with sweet tenderness. They continued touching and exploring, their movements an exquisite dance of new love and discovery.

Every touch, each taste of her skin, lit a flame of fire, sending shivers down her spine, every nerve dancing along the way. His hands roamed the curve of her hips, brushing the bare skin below, making her pulse race and her body shudder.

Their lips met in another scorching kiss filled with hunger and urgency, deepening as pure passion consumed them both. Heat filled the room as the sheer intensity of his mouth traced a searing line over her stomach, leaving a scorching path in its wake. It was all fire and desire as his mouth explored her body, devouring her, hitting all her sweet spots.

She trembled under his touch, and everything else in her life ceased to exist. Celine ignited, threading her fingers through his thick hair, her body arching at the stroke of his caress, releasing soft sounds of pleasure escaping her lips.

He lifted his head and met her gaze, staring deep. The gleam in his eyes went…molten. It was then that his head dropped, and his mouth hovered over hers for a fraction of a second before settling against hers.

Anthony's lips moved across hers with the tip of his tongue stroking the seam of her lips. And kissed her as if he couldn't get enough.

She fought to get closer. Her body ached with want. Celine kissed him back as heat flared within her, releasing a wild, primal need.

When he entered her, he did it slowly, allowing her body to drown in the sweet sensation of each stroke. She loved the feel of his mouth against hers and the long, hard feel of his body.

"You feel incredible," he moaned between kisses as he began to move, pulling back slowly, teasing her, tormenting himself.

Gazing into her eyes, he pushed into her deeper, making her his and filling her completely. Moving with an intensity, he gave her everything she wanted, everything she needed, unleashing all the power in his body and love in his heart in every movement.

Tonight, the stars aligned, and there was no holding back. She moved with him in a fiery, urgent passion in an endless moment of exquisite ecstasy of excruciating pleasure.

He brushed the side of her cheek with his lips as her breath caught, watching her face as she tipped over the edge, shattering her defenses, surrendering to him completely. A whirlwind of emotions followed, and he kissed her like she was his, now and forever. With Celine engulfed in his arms, he finally let go right behind her.

The night had been perfect. When they came together, it was better than she'd ever imagined, as powerful as anything she'd ever experienced. Celine reached out and stroked his face, marveling at the magic they created between them.

He leaned down to kiss her tenderly on the lips, pulling her in close to his side, and held her for a time until their breathing returned to normal.

As Celine snuggled in his arms, she took stock of her life. Since meeting Anthony, her life had changed for the better, bringing her to new heights that she couldn't have imagined.

He made her feel loved.

And in her heart, she felt hope.

"I have something for you," Anthony whispered.

She snuggled closer to him. "I have everything I need."

"Would you like it now or in the morning?"

"What is it?"

"I'll be right back." He winked and pulled on his pants and headed across the yard to his house.

When he returned minutes later, Anthony smiled and handed her a rectangular, flat box, gift wrapped in silver paper and a red ribbon. "Merry Christmas, Celine."

"You got me a present?"

"I have one for Savannah, too. I placed it under your Christmas tree."

"You're so sweet."

"Open it."

She untied the ribbon and removed the paper, revealing a dark blue velvet jewelry box. Lifting the lid, she stared at the exquisite heart-shaped sapphire pendant hanging from a sparkling gold necklace. "It's beautiful."

"It matches your eyes."

She turned her head slowly, meeting his gaze. "Thank you."

"Here, let me put it on you." Anthony took the delicate necklace and clasped it around her neck. "It looks beautiful. Like you."

"I wish I had a gift for you."

His gaze met hers and held. "I have you. You're my gift," he said, pulling her into his arms. "All I want is just you."

The cottage was quiet as Celine turned on her side and peeked at the time on her phone. It was four in the morning. She lay awake watching Anthony sleeping. Watched the rise and fall of his bronzed chest emblazoned with a tattoo of the USMC emblem of the eagle, globe, and anchor over his left pec. She itched to run her hand over it, but didn't want to wake him. He looked so peaceful, and yet so powerful and incredibly masculine.

It was strange waking up next to Anthony. Before, she had believed no man could ever measure up to her late husband. But knowing each relationship was different, her heart told her it wasn't fair to compare Anthony to Dex. Two different men, different circumstances.

Celine chose to move forward in her new life and risk her heart. If she hadn't, she might regret it for the rest of her life.

And now her life had changed.

As she fingered the delicate necklace around her neck and watched the gorgeous man beside her, she could no longer deny her deep feelings for him.

You made it easy for me to fall for you. How could I not?

"I can feel you watching me," Anthony whispered, opening one eye and glancing at her.

She curled up next to him. "Go back to sleep."

He rolled onto his side and wrapped her up in his arms. "Sleep is overrated." With a lazy smile on his face and his hair disheveled, he drew her fingers to his lips and kissed them. "Maybe we can find something else to do."

Celine blushed, turned her head, and looked up at him, unable to conceal her expression.

"You're smiling."

"I'm happy."

"And why are you so happy?"

Love ignited inside her heart. "Because I'm with you."

"Happy looks beautiful on you."

She ran her fingers over his chest and kissed him.

22

Bridget brought Savannah home along with two overflowing bags of zucchini, tomatoes, and apples.

"This is way more than I thought you'd bring me. What am I going to do with all of it?" Celine said, astonished at the amount of vegetables.

"Can most of the tomatoes in mason jars to use later. Peel and slice the apples and freeze them for any future pies you want to make."

"But the zucchini...there's so much."

"Make zucchini bread. They freeze well. You can always take a few loaves to the firehouse. Anthony and the guys would love it."

So that's what they did after Bridget left. While they baked, Savannah regaled her mother with a rundown of her time at the ranch, feeding chickens and horses.

"I picked out all the vegetables to bring home. When we finished, Andrew and Bridget took me for a horse ride. Afterwards, he let me help him brush his horse."

"It sounds like you had a wonderful time in the country."

"I love riding. Mommy, can I get a horse?"

A twinge of guilt squeezed her heart. "Sweetheart, we live in the city and there's nowhere for us to keep a horse."

"Can we move to the country?"

"Maybe someday. But for now, my job is in San Francisco. All your friends are here, and I'm sure you wouldn't want to leave them."

"I hadn't thought of that."

Celine and Savannah made a half dozen loaves of zucchini bread and put two aside to take down to the firehouse for the firefighters to enjoy.

On their way there, they stopped by Savannah's garden. Teddy had left her a note.

Dear Savannah,

I've received my new orders from Santa Claus. I wanted to let you know the exciting and sad news, that it's time for me to pack up and move back to the North Pole. I have loved getting to know you and your special Christmas garden through these gift exchanges. Your kindness towards others hasn't gone unnoticed. I hope you always think of me when you look at the red heart lucky charm. You are a wonderful little girl who has a special place in my heart. I'll never forget you.

Love, Teddy

"Mommy, Christmas is over. It's time to take the toys left in my garden to the homeless shelter. I bet some little boy or girl would like to have the gifts people left."

"I think that's a wonderful idea. We'll do it when we get home."

Anthony and his crew sat around the kitchen table inside the firehouse. Having a meal together was like having a meal with family. The guys at the station lived together half the year and were a family.

Watching Celine walk into the firehouse, he stopped his

conversation mid-sentence. She had her hair up in a ponytail and wore only mascara and lip gloss. Her eyes shined bright as the diamond studs in her earlobes. It was hard not to stare at the woman coming into the room. At times, she made him forget his own name.

"Celine." He pushed his chair out and stood, making his way toward her. "This is a nice surprise."

"Please don't get up. Savannah and I made zucchini bread. Too much for just the two of us. We thought we'd share."

"That was thoughtful of you. It smells delicious."

This close, she smelled much better than the bread, as the subtle scent of her perfume—like spun sugar with warm vanilla undertones—wrapped around him.

He introduced her to all the guys. They were friendly and welcoming.

"Anytime you want to bring us goodies is okay by me," one firefighter said, taking one loaf from her.

After letting Savannah sit in the firetruck, Anthony took Celine's hand, her fingers slipped between his effortlessly, and when she gave his hand a light squeeze, he smiled. He walked them outside and their gazes locked.

"I've been thinking about you all day," he said, recalling how she felt the night before when he made love to her, how he watched her face as she came apart in his arms.

She stepped close, then reached up and brushed her fingers along his cheek. "I'll see you later."

She and Savannah walked back to the cottage. The entire way, she kept asking herself if she was in love with him? It seemed hard to face the realization that it might be true. Until she was sure she'd keep it to herself, not ready to make any declaration.

The following day Celine cleaned the cottage and Savannah's

routine continued as normal as it could be. After she picked up Savannah from daycare, she told her she had a surprise for her. Something she also looked forward to. She had received a call from the contractor. They finished the house, and she could move back in.

Today was the day Celine longed for. Although she loved the little cottage in Anthony's backyard and being close to him, she was ready to live in her own home once again.

They walked into their home and set down their suitcases. As they approached the new kitchen, they both gasped. Celine stood in awe, having never imagined her kitchen could look like something straight out of a decor magazine. Sparkling white cabinets, polished granite countertops, new hardwood floors, and brand new stainless steel appliances. It was stunning.

"Mommy, our kitchen is so pretty!"

The kitchen was impressive, as were the white French doors that opened onto the outdoor patio. She thought it looked perfect.

"Look, Mommy!" Savannah pointed to right outside the patio door. Following her gaze to see what had captured her attention, Celine observed the hummingbird hovering and flitting at the feeder.

Only it wasn't the feeder that had been there before the fire. This was a new feeder. And there was a note attached to it.

The Aztecs believed that fallen warriors would be reincarnated as hummingbirds. This will ensure you'll always feel safe.

Bridget

"It's beautiful." Celine recalled seeing the hummingbird feeder she had originally had on the ground in pieces after the fire. Bridget had been with her that day. Celine had told her the significance of the hummingbird and how she had the feeder hanging inside the patio after Dex died. And now, she couldn't help but cry at what this thoughtful gift meant to her and Savannah.

Entering the empty cottage left Anthony miserable. He wandered around in the quiet. The closets were empty of their things. Celine had put fresh sheets on both beds. The place looked better after they left it than it had before they'd moved in. They'd filled the small cottage with life and love. When they were here, it felt cozy and warm. Now it seemed cold and confining. He'd gotten used to seeing them daily, and it felt like they'd been gone for a month instead of a day.

He kept thinking about her. After his wife had died, he hadn't looked at another woman. When enough time had passed, he'd gone out on a few dates with women, but couldn't see a future with any of them and gave up looking. He'd already been married to what he considered the perfect woman and didn't think he'd ever find love again.

Until Celine entered his life.

She was a loving mother and a kind woman. Her infectious spirit and generosity garnered his attention. She was sweet and made him laugh. With her, he saw a future. The love and life he could have with Celine.

After closing the door, he went to call her. They made plans for him to bring over Chinese food that evening. She was getting them settled back into their home and thanked him for the sweet gesture.

Celine and Anthony spent the rest of the week together during their time off from work. He had dinner with them every night that he wasn't on duty at the firehouse, often cooking for them, playing board games, watching movies together, and staying late into the night. Every moment they spent together brought them closer.

Life had never looked brighter and more promising.

23

Celine hadn't told Anthony she was stopping by. She hadn't planned on taking a walk to the firehouse until Savannah suggested taking some of the cookies they'd just baked to Anthony and his crew. They boxed up two dozen and walked the few blocks to the firehouse.

As she turned the corner and moved down the street, she glanced at the brick building that housed his engine company. Making their way around the building, she stopped in her tracks at the sight before her. Her mouth went dry. Her chest tightened.

He stood in the parking lot with his back turned to her, then turned slightly. Celine recognized his profile. Anthony. And he wasn't alone.

A stunning woman wearing a snug sweater and equally snug jeans stood there with him, smiling, her hand on his arm. An intimate gesture. The woman moved closer until there was barely a space for air between them.

Anthony pulled the woman into his arms in a warm embrace.

Celine's heart fell.

The woman leaned in and kissed him.

Celine's head spun. Then anger boiled within her. Another

woman? He played her, stringing her along, making her think he cared for her. And here he was with another woman in his arms. Kissing her!

It was too much. Every instinct was telling Celine to run.

Humiliated, she dropped the box of cookies to the ground, grabbed Savannah's hand, turned on her heels, and fled.

"Mommy! We haven't brought Anthony his cookies!"

Celine had to get away from him. Far away. The wind whipped her hair as they rushed back to their house. She told herself this was why she never should have involved herself with him. She hadn't been ready for anything serious and should have never given in. He led her on to think he cared for her. And she'd bought it and slept with him.

She felt like a fool. A foolish woman who had opened herself up to be used. This was the reason she would stay alone for the rest of her life. The only man who ever truly loved her had died. The rest were all after only one thing.

She wiped the tears from her face as she reached home and told Savannah to get her pajamas on as she closed the door behind her. Turning away, she couldn't let Savannah see her broken heart.

It wasn't until later, after she tucked her daughter into bed and crawled under her own comforter, she could let go and cry. Not a few tears, but a good, long, grievous cry. Having worried about Savannah's state of mind with all the tragedy they'd suffered, she'd kept things bottled up deep inside. Tonight, all of her hidden emotions broke through.

Celine had thought things were going so well with Anthony. She had admitted to herself that she cared deeply for him. Felt comfortable enough to open up, get to know him, bring him into Savannah's life. Their friendship had evolved into romance. She'd given herself to him in the most intimate form of trust.

The timing of her house remodel being finished couldn't

have been more right. After what she saw, there would be no way she could have gone back to his cottage.

She grabbed a tissue from her nightstand and blew her nose. Chastised herself for being so foolish to let him charm her into believing he had feelings for her. She was loath to admit she could get so jealous.

Because I have feelings for him.

Well, no more. She'd go back to her old life with only Savannah. Away from Anthony. It was over between them.

Anthony heard Savannah's voice call out to her mother. He turned and Celine's dark gaze met his for a brief half second before she grabbed Savannah's hand and rushed away. He called out to her, but she was ignoring him or was too far away to hear him.

"Dammit!"

"Do you know her?" This from Samantha, his sister-in-law, who stood beside him. The same woman he had hugged and kissed moments before.

"Yes. My girlfriend. She must have seen you kiss me."

"You should call her and explain."

"I should explain in person, but I can't leave the firehouse while I'm on duty."

Samantha placed her hand on his arm in a soothing gesture. "I can go by her house to reassure her I'm not a threat. Maybe smooth things over for you."

"I don't think that would be a good idea. It would be better to hear it from me. I'll call Celine."

"I'm sorry I messed things up for you. I just wanted to see you since I'm in town and see how you're doing."

He waved goodbye as Samantha drove away and pulled out his cell phone to call Celine. The call went straight to voicemail, forcing him to leave a message. "Will you call me so we can talk?"

He went inside the station, grabbed a bottle of water from the refrigerator, pulled out a chair in the kitchen, and sat down with a heavy sigh.

"You all right, Callahan?" his captain asked.

Anthony dropped his head back. "Just great."

"I noticed that good-looking woman who came by to see you. Wasn't the same one who has stopped by over the last month. Must be hard juggling two of them."

Anthony fixed him with narrowed eyes. "The woman who was here—Samantha—she's my sister-in-law. My dead wife's sister. So shut the fuck up about them. I don't want to hear one more word about Sam or Celine."

The captain's shoulders slumped. "Sorry, man. I didn't know. You need anything, let me know."

What he needed was to talk to Celine. Seeing the hurt on her face nearly killed him. He loved her with all his heart and she needed to hear the truth to what she saw. He called her again as he walked to his bunk in the sleeping quarters where he'd have privacy as the rest of the crew were in the dayroom watching a movie.

He reached her voicemail again. "Celine, please call me. What you saw wasn't anything."

Then he called his sister. They were friends, and maybe Bridget would know where Celine was.

Mid conversation, the call out tones blared through the loudspeakers followed by the dispatcher's voice. "Engine 16, Truck 16, Paramedic 42, Battalion 4, respond to a report of a structure fire…"

Before dispatch could give the address, Anthony hung up and rushed toward the apparatus room. More firefighters followed, pouring out of the dayroom to pull on boots and turnouts and jump on the engine and truck. The huge bay doors rolled up. The crew could hear multiple phone calls ringing over the loudspeaker with hoards of people calling in about the fire.

Anthony pushed all thoughts of Celine aside as he jumped on the rig. He had work to do. He'd see her and explain the next day when he went off duty.

"Battalion 4 on scene, two-story residential structure. Smoke showing. Call a second alarm. This will be Green Street IC."

Anthony's engine company arrived on scene moments later. The police department had streets blocked off and officers directed traffic away from the scene. An enormous cloud of black smoke billowed from the structure as he stepped off the engine. An orange glow of flames licked at the eaves. Other engine companies arrived within minutes.

Another crew pulled the hose from the back of the engine and connected it to the hydrant next door. Anthony strapped on his oxygen tank just as his captain yelled out to him. "Callahan! Johnson! Two kids are still inside, possibly on the second floor." His attention was drawn to the hysterical woman on the sidewalk. The mother.

Dammit!

The crews had several water lines on the fire battling for control. Wind whipped the flames as Anthony and Johnson rushed inside with another crew spraying water ahead of them.

They worked their way through the crowded interior. So much clutter everywhere. Using their flashlights and finding the stairs, they stayed low in the darkness, feeling their way to the bedrooms. A window on the second floor blew out, shaking the structure. Red fiery flames licked at the walls. Both men crawled on the floor, circling the perimeter of the room, searching for the children. After covering the entire room and finding it empty, they moved across the hall to the other room, repeating the search.

"Found one!" Johnson called out.

"Take him out. I'll finish the room." Adrenaline pumping, Anthony continued working his way around the room. The bell on his oxygen tank rang out, signaling he had little oxygen left. Time to go.

Where are you, kid?

Checking the closet, he found a small child under a pile of clothes when he heard an eerie moaning sound in the darkness. His tank bell continued to ring. Time was running out. His tank was empty. He scooped the child up and placed him over his shoulder, pushed up to his knees, making his way toward the stairs.

"Callahan, get out! The roof is ready to go!" the captain called out over the radio.

A firefighter met him at the stairs and took the child from him. As soon as the firefighter scooped up the child and turned away toward the exit, the sounds of wood splintering pierced through the roar of the fire. The ceiling gave another baleful creak and came down with a fury. Its force slammed Anthony to the ground. The weight of the impact buckled the stairs, sending it crashing to the first floor along with Anthony, trapping him underneath the rubble.

His mind blurred as he tried to reach for his radio. He couldn't move. The weight on top of him was too great. Sharp, shooting pain screamed from his chest.

Firefighters with high flow 2 1/2 inch hose lines continued knocking down the fiery flames. Additional crewmembers attempted to free Anthony from the collapsed structure.

"Callahan's down!" one firefighter shouted. The last words Anthony heard before he faded into the darkness.

24

There was a forceful knock on the door. It surprised Celine to see Bridget standing on the other side, looking flushed and out of breath.

"You don't answer your phone?" Bridget snapped.

"It's best I don't," she said, not knowing what else to say.

Celine stopped short when Bridget barged into her house. She closed the door behind her and studied Bridget. Her face was so similar to Anthony's. "My phone is in the other room. I'm ignoring it."

"Ignoring my brother? He said you wouldn't return his calls."

Celine shrugged, paused a beat, and finally admitted to it. "That's right. I really don't want to talk about it. Is that why you're here?"

"If you'd answer your phone, you'd know."

Celine flinched at the cool tone of Bridget's words. "There's nothing to say."

"There's much to say. It's about Anthony."

Celine turned away and looked down at her hands, recalling the scene she witnessed last night. Her heart weighed heavily. "I don't want to talk about him."

Bridget stepped forward, and there was an empathetic look

on her face. "He was upset when you didn't return his calls, so he called me to talk. He told me what happened. Who you saw with him at the firehouse."

Celine lifted her chin. "It's none of my business. Anthony has a right to his own life and to choose who he sees."

"It's important for you to hear the truth. The woman you saw with him was Samantha, his sister-in-law. She hadn't seen him since Lily's funeral and she stopped by to see how he was doing."

"It looked to me like they had no problem getting reacquainted."

"It's not like that. My brother was a mess after Lily died. He'd always been close with her family, but after her death, he blamed himself. He retreated into a shell of his old self and wouldn't have any contact with them. Lily's family was worried about him and that's why Samantha went to see him."

Celine's emotions conflicted inside her heart. Could she be mistaken, and what she saw was truly innocent?

"Listen to me. Nothing is going on between them."

"You sound sure of that."

"Trust me on this."

A sudden wave of emotion washed over Celine, wanting to believe it was true. She had a lot to process when it came to her own life. So many things were going through her mind. Thoughts of her own loss and how much she'd resisted Anthony at first. How he made her feel loved and cared for. The more time she spent with him, the harder she'd fallen. And now, her heart had broken when she saw him with Samantha. Heartsick, how was she going to move forward?

Bridget gently touched her arm. "It's only been recently that I've seen the old Anthony emerge. And it's because of you. He's in love with you. And I think you feel the same."

Tears welled in Celine's eyes. "I don't know what to do."

Bridget wrapped her arms around her. "Everything will work out. But right now, get your coat and purse."

"I will not go see him and grovel with an apology because I misread a situation."

"This isn't about what you saw last night at the firehouse." When Celine looked at her with confusion, she went on. "Halfway through our conversation, he got called out on a structure fire. Anthony's hurt. He's in the hospital. You must come with me."

Celine's eyes widened with shock. "What happened?"

"His air-pack ran out of oxygen during a rescue, and instead of leaving the structure like he should have, he stayed inside to find a little boy who was still inside. The ceiling collapsed on him. He took in a lot of smoke, has cracked ribs and a concussion, and some burns."

Celine's hand flew to cover her mouth. "My God!" she took a deep breath. "He'll be okay, though?"

Bridged shrugged, her face veiled with worry. "Right now, he's not doing well. I know he'll want to see you when he wakes up."

Celine bundled Savannah into her coat and gave her a book to bring along. She grabbed her keys and followed Bridget to her car.

Celine noted the group of firefighters wearing their turnouts loitering outside the emergency room doors when Bridget dropped her off.

"I'll park the car and meet you in his room."

She spotted one of Anthony's co-workers she'd met before leaning against the wall. She stopped and took a deep breath. "How is he?"

"Hard to say. They're only letting family in to see him."

"I'll see what I can find out and let you know."

She found his room easily. A sense of unease settled inside her as she stopped outside the room and gathered her courage. She took a deep breath and braced herself for what lay beyond the door.

Celine pushed the door open and stepped inside the stark white room, not sure what to expect. Someone had drawn the curtains. The room was as dim as a tomb. She stopped, wondering if she was in the right room. Before she could move, a man turned around. A handsome older version of Anthony with silver hair, cut in a flat-top style haircut, broad shoulders, and friendly ice-blue eyes.

"I'm sorry. I didn't mean to intrude. I'm looking for Anthony Callahan's room."

He moved slowly and held out his hand. "I'm Andrew, Anthony's father."

Anthony had told her about his father. Andrew, a retired Naval aviator and flight officer, was a powerful man with a razor-sharp mind, confident to the point of arrogant. He was also a computer coding genius who invented a high level security software program that earned him billions. While two of Anthony's brothers worked at the family firm, Anthony and Bridget preferred to follow their passion careers rather than sit behind a desk at their father's business.

"I'm Celine, a friend of Anthony's. Bridget dropped me off and went to park her car. She said it would be all right for me to come inside."

"Of course. Come in, Celine. Anthony is sleeping at the moment."

"How is he?"

"The roof collapsed and fell on him. He has a concussion. A piece of wood sliced a gash on the side of his neck, coming too close for comfort with his carotid artery. He's incredibly lucky. The doc stitched him up. He inhaled too much smoke, so they're going to keep him for several nights for observation. He's beat up."

Bridget came into the room with Savannah. "Dad, remember my student, Savannah, who came with me to the ranch? She's Celine's daughter."

He smiled broadly at the little girl. "Hello, Savannah. I so enjoyed your visit. I hope you'll come back to see me and my horses sometime."

She nodded and looked at Anthony. "Is Anthony hurt?"

"Yes, he's hurt, but I don't want you worrying. He needs some rest to feel better. Listen, I'm going to take a walk and get a coffee. Would you like to go to the cafeteria with me and get a cup of apple juice?" He turned toward Celine. "That is, if it's all right with your mother?"

"Mommy, please? I'm thirsty."

"Perhaps Bridget would like to go with us?" he asked, sensing Celine needed some time alone with his son.

Bridget met his eyes and understood his gentle hint. "I could use a coffee."

Andrew touched Celine's shoulder. "Can I get you anything?"

"I'm fine, thank you."

Once they'd left, Celine stepped forward to the bed, gazed down at Anthony, and covered his hand with hers. "Oh, Anthony." Her anger at him drained away. Tears stung her eyes. Seeing him in the hospital hooked up to oxygen and monitors brought her back to the day when Dex had died. She couldn't go through that again. Her heart sank.

But Anthony wasn't Dex.

The past several weeks of her life with this man flashed before her. All she could think about was his gentleness, the way he laughed and smiled, the twinkle in his eyes when he looked at her. How his arms felt around her.

The way he loved her.

For a moment, she couldn't breathe, couldn't think. For a

moment, she could only feel. She lowered her gaze and watched the rise and fall of his chest, which held the most loving, caring heart she'd ever known. Her hand shook as she wound her fingers through his, her heart breaking seeing him so badly injured.

"You have to be all right. I can't lose you now that I've found you," she confessed, before closing her eyes. "You can't die. There's so much I need to tell you." It struck her then, just how much he meant to her. Until this moment, she hadn't realized how much she loved him.

She struggled to contain her emotions and maintain her composure, not realizing Bridget had returned until she moved to her side and placed an arm around her shoulders. "He'll be okay. My brother is one of the toughest men I know."

Bridget's soothing voice was a sharp contrast as Celine crumbled on the inside, trying to remain strong. Falling apart wouldn't help Anthony or his family. His injuries affected not only Celine, but his entire family as well.

"Come on, let's get you home and let Anthony get some rest. We can come back tomorrow," Bridget said.

It was hard to leave him. How would she know if something changed, and he took a turn for the worse? She wanted to be here with him when he woke up.

As if reading her mind, Bridget spoke up. "Dad is going to be here all night. He'll call me if anything changes."

"And you'll call me?"

"Of course. I'm going to step outside and talk to Dad."

Celine nodded, unable to speak. She leaned over Anthony and pressed a gentle kiss on his forehead.

25

Anthony awakened to the sound of the repetitive beeping of a heart monitor. He tried to force his eyes open. The effort sent a blaze of pain shooting through his head. He blinked his eyes, but his eyelids felt heavy, like lead. Through narrow slits, he looked up at the stark white ceiling. His eyes slowly scanned the room, saw the white walls, rails on the bed. He noted the IV taped to his left wrist. He was in the hospital.

Dark hair peeked out from under a blanket covering a slight figure who appeared to be sleeping, curled up in a chair near the bed. Bridget?

With immense effort, he looked to the window to his right. A dark sky loomed with the threat of rain. The effort was too much, and he closed his eyes.

Memories were coming back to him. The fire. Searching for a small child. Lifting a child into his arms and carrying him through the darkness. Then…nothing.

He reached up to his neck and felt the bandage. More bandages covered his cheeks. His entire body hurt. Alerted by movement and a breathy sound drew his attention to the chair. It was hard to open his eyes, but he kept on trying.

A warm hand wrapped around his. "Welcome back, Anthony. Go slowly."

The soft voice curled around him. Celine? He managed to open his eyes a bit more. Took in the worried look on her face. She had tired smudges under her eyes. "Celine," he whispered. A slow half-smile hinted at his mouth.

"I'm here. I'm not going anywhere."

He curled his hand around hers.

"You have a head injury. The doctors want you to rest for a few more days."

"What happened?"

"A ceiling collapsed on you during the fire. It knocked you out, and you have a nasty concussion. You'll hurt for a while."

He struggled to sit up and winced in pain. Attempting to sit up took incredible effort, and he finally gave up.

She put her hand on his shoulder with a soft touch. "Not yet. You have a couple of cracked ribs and need to rest so you can heal. I can get the nurse to give you some pain meds."

"Later. You're all I need."

At that moment, a nurse pushed through the door. "Good morning, Mr. Callahan. I'm happy to see you're awake. How do you feel?"

"Like a truck hit me."

She wrapped a cuff around his arm and checked his blood pressure, then adjusted his oxygen canula. "Vitals look good. How's the pain?"

"I'll live."

"Don't be a tough guy. The meds will help."

"Listen to her," Celine added.

"Fine. It's too hard to argue with two bossy women."

Celine and the nurse exchanged a look, grinning at each other.

"I'll be right back." The nurse left and returned a few minutes later with a paper cup with a few pills inside. "Take these."

After she left, Celine refilled his water and fluffed up his pillow. "Can I do anything for you?"

"Another blanket would be nice."

She grabbed one from the closet and covered him, smoothing her hand over it and tucking it around him before covering his hand with hers. "Better?"

"Thanks." Her hand was warm, reassuring. "How long have I been here?"

"A few days."

Her gentle touch pushed through a memory to his consciousness. She'd been with him here in the hospital. "When did you get here?"

"As soon as Bridget told me. I've been worried about you."

"I'm better now that you're here."

She blinked back tears. "You scared me."

"Sorry."

She wiped the tears from her eyes.

"Don't cry." He held out his hand for her. "Come here. Lay down with me."

"You have to be careful. I don't want to hurt you."

"You could never hurt me."

"You need sleep."

"Stay with me, then I'll sleep."

Celine carefully settled herself on the bed beside him, mindful of his injuries.

He drew her against him and closed his eyes, letting the pain meds sink into his bones. Relaxed and comfortable. A quiet moment soothing to his soul. No words were spoken, but so much was said. The woman in his arms was all he needed to soothe the pain. Anthony fell asleep holding her close, feeling her love, and gaining his peace.

26

A few close friends could visit Anthony the next day. The family whose house burned stopped by and thanked Anthony for rescuing their sons and fighting so bravely.

When Celine showed up at the hospital, Samantha and another woman were there inside Anthony's room. Anthony held out his hand to her. "Celine, I'd like you to meet Samantha, my sister-in-law, and her wife, Sasha."

Her wife?

The introduction momentarily stunned her. Her face reflected as much.

"Samantha stopped by the firehouse the night of the fire to share the good news she had recently married," Anthony said.

Samantha leaned forward and held out her hand to Celine. "It is so nice to meet you. Anthony has told us so much about you. I know my sister would be happy knowing what a wonderful woman you are."

"Congratulations on your marriage." Celine felt like such a fool for misconstruing what she had seen that night.

"We'll get out of your hair so you can get some rest. Let us know if you need anything," Samantha said to Anthony before leaving.

Before the door could fully close, Bridget and Savannah entered the room with Andrew and two other men. "Celine, meet our brothers, Christian and Rob. Christian is my twin."

"Yes, the more serious twin. Be careful around my sister and don't let her lead you astray. She is the wild child. The rebel," Christian said with a grin.

"I'll try to remember that," Celine replied, meeting Bridget's playful eyes.

"How are you feeling, son?" Andrew asked.

"Ready to get out of here and go home," Anthony said.

"I spoke to your doctor, and he recommended you stay a few more days until you can get around better."

"Yeah, we'll see," Anthony said, before turning toward Celine. "Can you pour me some water, please?"

"Of course." She poured him some from the pitcher in the room, added a straw, and helped him sit up.

"Thanks."

"Anthony, if you can't pour your own water, you'll need more help than you think. Either stay here and do what the doctor orders, or I'll arrange private home care nurses for you at home. It's your choice," Andrew said with a tone more in line with an order than a suggestion.

"Dad, I'm thirty-four years old and can make my own decisions."

"I don't think you should be alone at home. You could have a setback and injure yourself again. I'll take care of paying for the care if that's what you're worried about," Andrew insisted.

"I'm a grown man and don't need a babysitter," Anthony argued.

Celine and Anthony exchanged a look.

Celine spoke up. "Andrew, I'm a nurse and can check on him after my shift. You have my word he won't overdue it."

"That's perfect," Anthony agreed. "Celine can come over in

the evenings after she gets off work to help me out until I feel one-hundred percent."

"Anthony, you need round-the-clock care. Celine could always move in with you until you're back on your feet," Andrew suggested.

"I think that's a great idea," Bridget said with barely veiled enthusiasm. "Problem solved."

Andrew turned toward Celine. "My dear, if you could arrange with your job to take the time off from work, I will pay you double your salary to look after this stubborn bear of a son and make sure he doesn't crack any more ribs."

Celine stood there, feeling slightly awkward and wondering how she'd suddenly gotten talked into moving in with him, even if only temporarily. "I can't do that. I've used all my vacation time and can't get any more time off, even if I agreed."

"I'm sure we can work something out. If they give you any guff, let me know. I'm on the Board here at the hospital and can use my influence if necessary," Andrew added.

"Evenings are the best I can do without jeopardizing my job." Celine stared wide eyed at Anthony, shaking her head, clearly not enjoying being bullied by his father.

"Back off, Dad. This is one time your position and title won't get you what you want," Anthony said.

Father and son stared at each other for a long moment.

"Whatever you wish," Andrew conceded.

"We'll work around your schedule," Anthony assured Celine.

Savannah moved toward her mother then. "Mommy, can I give Anthony my present?"

Celine smiled down at her daughter, welcoming the distraction. "I think he'd like that."

"Hello, Savannah. I'm happy to see you," Anthony said with a soft voice.

She handed him a small gift wrapped in red tissue paper. "I brought you something to help you heal. I hope you like it."

He took the gift from her and held her eyes. "I know I will." Carefully pulling the tissue paper away, he held the small red lucky charm. He stared at it, aware of its significance.

"Teddy the elf gave it to me. It made me feel better and I hope it makes you feel better," she said.

Anthony held out his arms. "Come here, little one."

Celine lifted Savannah onto the bed and she eased into his embrace.

"Thank you, Savannah. It is so incredibly sweet of you to share your special gift with me. I'm feeling better already." He kissed her cheek and cradled her in his arms. His eyes were wet when he let her go.

Bridged sensed they needed some time alone to talk over what their father had proposed about his care after he left the hospital. "Celine, Christian and I are going out for ice cream. Would it be okay if Savannah came with us? I can bring her home afterwards."

"Mommy, please," Savannah begged.

"I think that would be fun. Thank you." Celine handed Bridget her spare house key.

"We'll be back in the morning," Christian said before leaving. "Hopefully, they'll spring you. If not, let me know. I'll bring you something better than hospital food."

After a few more minutes, Anthony's family left.

He turned to Celine and held out his hand. "Come sit next to me." When she sat beside him, he picked up her hand and his fingers curled around hers. His eyes softened. "We need to talk. About that night."

She chewed on her bottom lip, trying to figure out what to say. Her heart turned over with a mix of emotions. He was making her feel so many things. "Seeing you with her, hugging her...and when I saw her kiss you, it broke my heart."

"Let me explain."

Celine stared at the back of her hand. "I'm not sure I want to hear it."

"Don't you think you're being a bit harsh? Dammit, Celine, hear me out."

Celine's head jerked up, and she looked him in the eye, knowing she must move past it. "You're right. I'm sorry."

"After Lily died, I avoided her family. Lily and Samantha look so much alike. It was too painful for me to be around her. I'd brushed off Samantha and hadn't seen her in years. There's nothing between us except friendship. She surprised me at the firehouse to let me know she'd gotten married. To Sasha."

"I know that now. I just assumed when I saw her..."

He cut her off. "You assumed wrong. Watching you walk away gutted me."

Celine squeezed her eyes shut, frustrated with herself for leaving the way she did. She realized now she shouldn't have done that and tried to shake any lingering negative thoughts from her mind.

A heavy silence fell between them.

She glanced at his hand on top of hers. "I'm sorry I jumped to the wrong conclusion. It's just...we moved so fast and I wasn't ready for you or how fast everything between us happened."

His expression softened. "My heart was ready for you. Why don't we agree we both could have handled it better?"

She closed her eyes, overwhelmed by emotion because he was right.

"You don't know what you do to me." He touched the curve of her jawline with his fingertips. "You are everything to me. I can't imagine living a second of my life without you beside me."

"I'm not sure I know how to do this."

"Look at me, Celine. I'm in love with you."

On the verge of tears, she stared at him, afraid to admit her feelings.

"I love you. It's true." His heart pounded at what those three words meant. "I love your spirit, your kindness, everything about you. And I know you love me."

She didn't say a word for a long moment.

"Don't push me away, Celine." He lifted her chin and made her look at him. "Tell me you don't feel the same way. Tell me you don't feel the love and passion between us when I make love to you."

She had tears in her eyes. "I don't know how I feel…"

His eyes searched hers. "Yes, you do. You're a woman who knows what you want but is afraid to admit it to yourself. You feel it too. I can see it in your eyes."

Celine was silent so long Anthony didn't think she was going to answer.

His admission of love hit her with startling clarity. She'd already lost her heart to Anthony. Tears ran down her cheeks. "You see it because it's true. I am in love with you."

Anthony opened his mouth to speak, but she held her hand up and shook her head.

"I'd convinced myself I'd grow old alone. And then you walked into my life. I never planned to fall in love with you. But I did. You make me feel things I'd given up on ever feeling again. And it scared me to death when I saw you here in the hospital hooked up to IVs and monitors, afraid I would lose you."

At the look in his eyes, her heart nearly stopped. "I can't lose you."

He swallowed hard as he took her in. It was almost more

than he could take. "If your lips don't touch mine soon…you might just kill me."

"Anthony…"

Anthony cut off her words with his mouth as he pulled her into his arms, taking her by surprise and bringing her into a possessive embrace. His lips were warm and gentle, soothing her worried heart. Tenderness, longing, and love swept through them.

Their eyes connected, and unbridled love bound them together. Her heart told her to hold tight and never let go.

"I'm grateful to be alive and here with you. I love you. Nothing else matters."

He held her against his chest, running his fingers through her hair. Gently, he said, "You are the woman who owns my heart, my love. Only you."

Inhaling his scent this close calmed her. The warmth of his touch and the love in his voice made the tension between them evaporate. He was making her feel so many things she never thought she'd feel again. Relief flooded her as love filled her.

It was a long time before she lifted her head and looked into his eyes. "And you, Anthony, have my heart."

27

In the weeks since being released from the hospital and recuperating at home, Celine had been a comforting presence. Once the home care nurse his father hired left for the day, Celine and Savannah would come to Anthony's house after she got off work and picked up Savannah from daycare.

Celine was adamant about him not doing anything too taxing. They'd cook for him, watch television together, and made plans to take Savannah to Disneyland once he'd healed.

Fighting headaches and soreness in his ribcage as if a bus had hit him, Anthony's bruised body still held the physical marks of the result of a ceiling crashing down on him. He tried to brush off the injuries and move about the house as normal, but Celine could see him fighting the pain. She took charge and forced him to rest in bed or on the sofa. He'd try to get her to join him in bed. She nixed that idea. No sex until she was satisfied he was fully recovered. There was no arguing with her.

She arrived early on her day off, sent the nurse home, and moved to the kitchen to make him lunch. When he hobbled in, he saw her standing at the counter, wearing a pair of jeans and a pink shirt that clung to her curves. He met her gaze, and she smiled, sending his heartbeat racing. He immediately drew her in with his blue eyes.

"Where's Savannah?" he asked, moving closer.

"A friend's house. She's having a slumber party."

"So, she won't be home until...?"

"Tomorrow."

A grin tugged at the corners of his mouth. His mind went straight to one thing. He moved closer, touched her hip and left his hand there, wanting to take advantage of the moment. "That means we have the house to ourselves."

Her cheeks flushed pink, and for an instant she was... entranced.

He looked down at the sandwich makings on the counter. "All of this is wonderful, but there's something I want more than food."

His hand lingered, and he pulled her against him, drawing in a ragged breath as time seemed to stop. Then she lifted those soft blue eyes, their gazes entwined, and sent him a look he was fast becoming addicted to.

Anthony trailed the back of his hand down her jaw. "You are so beautiful."

"Anthony?"

"I missed you." He smiled at her, slow and sexy, with the overwhelming desire to feel his mouth on hers. "I want to kiss you."

She lifted her left brow and took a step closer. "I want you to kiss me."

Her heady perfume mixed with her scent was intoxicating, unleashing a visceral need to love her, to inhabit the depths of her body, her soul. His head dipped, his mouth inches above hers. "I can't stay away from you any longer." He leaned into the kiss. Light, tentative, slow and easy. His body stirred against hers. And didn't go unnoticed.

"You're still recuperating. That means you are to relax and not exert yourself."

"I'm dying a slow death here, not able to touch you."

She tilted her head back and smiled at him. "Do as I say," she whispered against his ear, tugging his shirt from his jeans and unzipping him.

Before he could reply, she had her hand wrapped around the hard length of his erection and was stroking him. He sucked in a breath. "Fuck, Celine," he groaned.

"My plans exactly." She slowly dragged him into his bedroom. "Now lie back." She took off her shirt. Her black lace bra left little to his imagination.

"You're such a little minx. I like this idea."

She had him spread out on the bed, an amused expression covering his face. "I am yours to ravish as you wish."

She stripped off her clothes. The sight of her gorgeous body had him struggling to maintain control. He needed to feel her against him, loving him, and wanted to spend the rest of his life memorizing her every curve.

Celine leaned in to kiss him. He closed his eyes as she started working her way down his body, one kiss at a time. Her lips trailed a path to his chest, leaving a slow line of wet kisses to his stomach. His body trembled at the heat igniting every cell.

It wasn't until she positioned herself over him, straddling his hips and teasing his cock, did their eyes meet and hold. Nothing else existed, except at this moment. At the look in her eyes, he groaned, leaving him fighting for control.

She smiled provocatively and sunk down on him. He filled her completely. A low moan escaped her. The moment felt endless, satisfying, as if coming home at last.

"Good God, just kill me now and I'll die a happy man."

"Not yet," she whispered, and began to move.

They made love slowly and tenderly. He moved with her at the pace she set, drawing out his want, his need for release, the unbearable sweet torture of intense pleasure pushing him closer to the edge. Though he wanted to go slowly, he found he couldn't. He was panting, unable to hold back any longer.

Her teeth grazed over her bottom lip and Anthony's caveman instincts took over, thrusting his hips deeper, every nerve on fire. He held both her hips as she writhed on top of him. Her breath hitched in her throat as waves of pleasure coursed through her body, surrendering to the magic they created, and sending his world shattering to a crescendo, losing himself in her arms.

He pulled her to his side and held her, catching his breath. Her dark hair fell in disheveled waves around her face, a warm afterglow of just having incredible sex reflected in her eyes. His heart pounded, and her intoxicating scent swirled around him, reminding him of how good it felt to have her with him in his bed. "I don't want you to go home, Celine."

"I don't have to tonight."

"Not only tonight. Ever." Celine had captivated his heart the moment she entered his life. She'd left him crazy for her and he didn't want her to be anywhere else but here with him.

Without hesitating, he leaned over and kissed her. "I love you. We love each other. You, me, Savannah...we can be a family." He searched her face, hoping she'd feel the same way about what he was about to ask her. "I want to be the one you curl up with at night. To have you fall asleep in my arms. Sell your house and move in with me."

Listening to him wanting a life with her brought tears to her eyes. "I can't do that. We can't live together. Setting a good example for Savannah is important to me."

A subtle smile crossed Anthony's face. He ran his fingers gently along her cheek. "Then marry me."

28

"Marry you? You want to get married?"

His eyes met hers, filled with promises of a future. "There's something beautiful between us. You're so special to me. I want you here with me, where I can love you for the rest of our lives." He lifted her hands to his mouth and kissed them. "I want to marry you. Take a chance with me."

Her heart caught. She blinked back the emotion. So much had happened between them. So many changes to their lives. Celine never thought she could find another man as kind and loving as Dex. The world had a funny way of proving her wrong. Life had given her happiness not only with Dex, but a second chance at love with Anthony.

Savannah loved Anthony. Celine did too, falling deeper in love with every passing moment, more than she ever could have imagined. He was thoughtful and kind and had a caring heart filled with love. Everything she could hope for in a man.

Her eyes filled with tears. The love she had with Anthony was real and true. She knew a good man when she saw him. Anthony had been a gift of love sent to her when she needed him most. She wanted to be with him. Now was the time to move forward and embrace the future. A life and family with

Anthony. That was what he had become for her.

Home.

"I never knew I could find love again." She touched his cheek with her fingertips, careful to avoid his bandage, and gazed deep into his eyes. "But I have with you."

"And?"

She pressed a tender kiss on his lips, dropped her hand on his chest and felt his strong heart beat against her. Breathing in the scent of him as the warmth of his love surrounded her, she smiled. "Yes, I'll marry you."

Anthony pulled her against his chest and wound his arms around her as if he were afraid to let go. He bent his head and kissed her slowly, thoroughly. "I'm going to have a few burn scars," he said between kisses.

Celine tipped her head back to look into Anthony's face.

He looked down at her and ran his fingers over the bandage on his jaw. "Will it bother you?"

"What matters to me is what's inside your heart. Yours overflows with kindness and love. Although, I will say your scars will give you an edgy bad-boy look." The corners of her mouth curled in the dim light of the room. "Which I kind of like."

He raised his left brow. "Why don't you show me how much you love bad-boys?"

"Now that you've exhausted me, I'm starving. Let's find some food." Anthony swung his legs over the bed and stood.

Celine made them scrambled eggs, bacon, and slices of sourdough bread toast with a thick layer of strawberry jam.

"You're spoiling me." Anthony sent her an appreciative look as she set their plates on the table and sat down next to him.

"I don't mind." She loved having her cooking enjoyed.

"Firemen are known for their cooking skills, but you, my dear, give us a run for our money." He looked up at her with affection. "Once I'm better, I look forward to creating some culinary masterpieces with you in our kitchen."

Our kitchen. The words warmed her heart. This was really happening. She loved this man and looked forward to living with him and making a life together. She looked at him from across the table, and he sent her a wink.

They spent the next twenty-four hours curled up on the couch watching movies with Tucker curled up on Anthony's lap or in bed, satisfying Anthony's insatiable appetite for her.

Celine was so happy with Anthony at his home that she didn't want their alone time to end. She finally had to put decent clothes on and make herself presentable to pick up Savannah from her friend's house so it wouldn't look as if she just rolled out of bed.

Before she left, he caught her hand and brought it to his mouth, pressed his lips against her palm. "You know something, Celine? I can't wait to marry you."

His words tugged at her heart. "I feel the same way."

He said nothing for a long moment, too busy looking at her. The corner of his mouth lifted, and he ran his fingers down her cheek. "And when you're ready, let's make a baby."

"You want a baby?"

"I do. What about you? Would you consider having more children?"

"I've always wanted Savannah to have a sibling."

"That makes me happy to hear."

"How many do you want?"

He brushed his lips against hers. "As many as you'll have."

29

Saratoga was a charming little town located only an hour south of San Francisco, on the outskirts of world famous Silicon Valley. Many tech executives called it home. An affluent area filled with expensive homes, and well known for its wineries and restaurants.

Celine fell in love with this hidden small-town gem. Shoppers lingered over steaming cups of cappuccino on outdoor patios of coffee shops. Art galleries, boutiques, and small businesses made up the village of the downtown.

As they drove, she caught views of the steep rolling hills that extended beyond the town. It was difficult for Celine to bring her eyes away from the stunning scenery outside the truck's window. A family of deer stood off to the side of the road eating berries from a bush. She rolled her window down. The clean air filled her lungs. So far away from the city smog, it smelled fresh and intoxicating. Making their way into the Saratoga foothills amid vineyards covering gently rolling hills, the area reminded her of the Napa Valley.

Anthony turned at the stone pillars with the steel gated entrance onto the private cobblestone road that led to his father's home.

Celine's head was spinning, driving in the middle of a

sprawling expanse of vineyards on either side of the long driveway. She caught sight of the *ranch house,* graced within a never ending meticulously landscaped scenic backdrop. In her mind, a ranch house out in the country would be a single story rustic structure with a barn. This home was anything other than rustic.

What stood before her was an enormous, one of a kind Tuscany-inspired equestrian and vintner estate on acres of total tranquility away from the hustle and bustle of the city. The grounds were gorgeous, breathtaking, offering privacy and serenity.

"This is your father's country house?" she asked as they pulled up and parked.

"The ranch house. That's what he likes to call it. He built it when he was tired of living in the city. Bridget lives in his San Francisco home."

"Wow. It isn't what I was expecting."

"It's a bit over the top for my taste."

"It's beautiful."

"Personally, I don't understand why he built so large a home. It's not like his family lives with him. He lives alone. We all have our own homes."

There were several cars and trucks parked in front of the garage, and Celine looked over at Anthony. "Is your father having a party?"

He opened her door for her, gave her a smile, and took her hand. "A little family gathering," he mused, and led her across the driveway to the front door. He rang the doorbell to give fair warning, and before anyone answered, he opened the door and they stepped inside the foyer.

"Dad, we're here," he called out, closing the door behind him. Two large dogs greeted him, dancing around his feet, happy to see him. Then they ignored him and went straight to Savannah, licking her face and wagging their tails as if they remembered her from her previous visit.

"This is Rhett," Anthony said as he ruffled the German Shepherd's head. "And this beautiful lady is Scarlett," he added, referring to the dark red Golden Retriever begging for Savannah's attention.

"Someone is a fan of *Gone With The Wind*?" Celine asked with amusement.

"It was my mother's favorite movie. She'd had a crush on Clark Gable since she was a teenager."

"We're in the great room," Bridget called out to her brother.

Savannah ran ahead, following Bridget's voice. Anthony took Celine's hand and led her down the hallway, passing through an arched doorway into the great room.

Celine's eyes scanned an enormous room with a fire blazing brightly in an impressive fireplace flanked by stonework and dark wood. Two leather sofas faced each other in front of the fireplace, separated by a custom made coffee table made with an enormous slab of oak taken from a tree on the property that had the misfortune of being uprooted during a storm.

Several sitting areas with cognac colored leather club chairs dotted the room, arranged in cozy clusters. A wall of windows flooded the room with light and showcased acres of green pasture where several horses grazed.

A beautiful kitchen with warm wood cabinets and granite countertops opened to the great room. The sheer size of the space was astounding.

Anthony's brother, Christian, moved forward, greeting them with a welcoming hug. "You're late. Dad wasn't sure if you would show."

"Caught a bit of traffic. Sharks game got out at the same time we came down the highway."

"Let's catch a game when they get back from their road trip," Christian suggested.

"Count me in."

Andrew entered the room. He smiled as his gaze swept over Celine and he pulled her into his arms. "Welcome. I'm so happy you're here with Anthony."

"Thank you for including us."

Andrew led her to a comfortable sofa where they sat and stretched out their legs. Bridget brought them both a cappuccino.

"Thank you, my dear," Andrew said with affection to his daughter before turning to Celine. "I've developed a fondness for Miss Savannah since Bridget brought her to the ranch. I missed out on much of my own children's childhood when they were young when I deployed with the Navy. Having a little one around brings me immense joy."

Celine cradled her coffee in her hands and nodded in agreement. "Children are why I work in pediatrics. They fill my heart."

"Now that my son is out of the hospital, it's time to celebrate."

Celine watched as Rob threw another log into the fireplace, where a fire crackled in the hearth. She leaned close to Andrew. "Your son has made this a memorable Christmas for Savannah. I can't thank him enough," she said in a soft voice.

"Savannah and Bridget told me about *Teddy*. Anthony's heart has always been in the right place."

Bridget came into the room. "Dinner is ready."

Andrew stood and offered Celine his hand to help her from the sofa. She caught Anthony's eye and his look of approval when Andrew placed his hand on the small of her back and led her into the kitchen.

The relaxed meal passed in a blur as everyone gathered in the enormous kitchen to eat the delicious barbecue Rob and Christian had grilled for the group. Bridget had an array of fresh fruits, cheeses, macaroni and cheese, and other kid friendly foods for Savannah.

After they finished eating, Andrew and Christian took Savannah over to the stables to feed carrots to the horses. Celine helped Bridget clean up while Anthony caught up with Rob by the fire.

When the girls finished, Bridget suggested Anthony show Celine the guest house where she and Savannah would stay. "I thought it would offer privacy. This big house may be overwhelming for Savannah."

Anthony rose and looked around for Celine's luggage.

"I placed it inside the guesthouse. Wasn't sure if you would be able to manage it as you're still convalescing," Rob said.

Anthony gave his brother a look. "I'm fine. But thanks."

They wandered past the swimming pool and made their way down the stone path toward the guesthouse. Once inside, Celine stopped and became momentarily distracted, admiring the extravagant accommodations. A large living room with stone walls with leaded windows looked out over acres of vineyards. A granite fireplace dominated the room, and there was a plush sofa and several chairs arranged in front of the fireplace.

"This is beautiful."

"Not as beautiful as you." Strong arms curled around her waist, drawing her back against him. He dipped his head and pressed a warm kiss against that tender spot at the juncture of her neck and shoulder. "Have I told you how much I love you?"

His touch made her catch her breath. She turned in his arms and leaned into him, lifting a hand to his cheek, then roaming along his jawline. "Not nearly enough."

His mouth claimed hers in a slow journey, tasting her lips, down her throat, drinking her in. She closed her eyes, breathing him in and he pulled her tight against him, kissing her thoroughly until she was breathless and her legs grew weak.

He pulled away and grinned. "You're making it impossible to stop kissing you."

She wanted this man, now more than ever. "I wish you could stay here with me."

He laughed. "It won't be hard to sneak into your room." He pressed a kiss on her forehead.

"Where are you sleeping?"

"The other guest house."

"There's another one?"

"Next door. Dad just finished it. It's much smaller than this one."

The sound of voices outside grew closer before there was a rap on the door. Anthony moved to open the door, and Andrew and Savannah stepped inside.

"How are your accommodations?" Andrew asked Celine.

"I feel spoiled. Like I'm staying at a high end hotel villa."

Her comment made Andrew smile. "I love to have my children visit me. I also understand how they each like their privacy. Having the guest houses ensures they will come visit more often without old dad here constantly hovering."

"Dad likes his guests to be comfortable and feel at home," Anthony added.

"There should be coffee in the cupboard for the morning. Please join us for breakfast in the main house at nine. Let Anthony or any of us know if there's anything you need."

"Thank you, Andrew. It's more than enough."

"Mommy, where will I sleep?" Savannah asked.

"I'll show you in just a few minutes."

After they unpacked, Celine pulled her black wool peacoat tightly around her and bundled Savannah up in her red fur jacket before they joined the family on the large stone patio in the backyard. A tall outdoor heater helped to take the chill from the air. Christian lit a fire in the fire pit, adding more warmth to the cool winter evening. Bridget brought out ingredients to make s'mores, and Andrew helped Savannah roast marshmallows for the campfire treat.

Anthony draped his arm across Celine's shoulders as they sat on the comfortable outdoor loveseat. He leaned close to her ear. "My father is in his element. For several years now, he's pestered the four of us for grandchildren."

"Savannah is enjoying his attention. She misses having her grandparents close by."

It wasn't long before everyone had eaten their share of s'mores and darkness had fallen on the relaxing evening. The two dogs curled up with Savannah on a massive lounge chair and in no time, she had fallen asleep. Andrew doted on her, placing a cozy afghan over her.

Celine finished the last of her wine and set the glass down on the table. "I should get her to bed. She's had a long day."

"I'll carry her," Anthony said, standing up.

"I've got her, son. Those cracked ribs of yours are still healing," Andrew said, gently lifting the sleeping girl in his arms and following them back to the guest cottage.

Anthony waited for Celine near the fireplace while she tucked Savannah in bed. "She asleep?"

"Your father wore her out with all the *horse chores* he gave her."

He grinned. "Feeding and petting horses can be exhausting."

Celine took his hand and led him outside. "I love it here. You never see stars like this in the city." The glow from the stars and full moon was the only illumination.

Anthony looked up at the glittering sky. "Out here in the country affords you a better view of life."

"It's a beautiful night." A shiver ran through her. "A cold, beautiful night." Standing in the sweet night air, he swept her up in his powerful arms and held her close. She leaned back against his chest. His warm breath tickled her neck.

"Absolutely beautiful," he whispered. Lifting her hair aside and lightly trailing his lips over her skin, he pressed a soft kiss to the curve of her neck. He ran his hands down her arms, soaking in the silky softness of her skin. "This is the best part of my day. Time alone with you."

Celine closed her eyes, enjoying the feel of him and his hands roving over her curves. It seemed natural to curl in his arms and kiss him. The light and tender kiss soon turning greedy, his hungry mouth devouring her lips. Her breath caught in her throat when he broke the kiss and stared at her.

The smoldering desire in his eyes barely concealed his illicit thoughts. "Never have I wanted anyone the way I want you." He leaned down, his mouth covering hers in a searing kiss. Pulling her closer, he deepened the kiss, causing a jolt to spiral through her.

He ran his thumb along her lower lip. "I could kiss you all night."

Her dark blue eyes lifted, revealing similar thoughts of her own pent-up longing. "You have a few hours until Savannah wakes up." She took him by the hand and led him to her bedroom, locking the door behind her.

His heart pounded in his chest. "What do you have in mind? Savannah is right in the other room."

"Then we'll have to be very, very quiet," she said, running her hands up his chest. "If you want to, that is."

"Woman, you are playing with fire." A low growl came from deep inside him at the thrill her words gave him. "Just try to keep me away from you."

His fingers dug into her hips and pulled her closer. "I'm going to make you want to scream, but you can't make a sound."

"Don't make promises you can't keep," she teased.

With a devilish glint in his eyes, he studied those lips of hers. "I'll have you whimpering, begging before I'm done loving you."

Before she could take a breath, Anthony tilted her chin and pressed his lips against hers. A tender, lingering kiss full of passion. A kiss that spoke volumes.

Her arms wound around his neck, and he deepened the kiss, pulling her down on the bed. In tune with her body, he took his time, sliding his lips across her skin. Delicate kisses, dangerously slow and heated heralded passionate ones, leaving her quivering under his warm breath. His lips slow danced over her skin, savoring her, drinking in all she offered, arousing her most sensuous desire.

Primal energy bristled off his body. The fire of his lips brought her body to life. A shiver ran through her being loved so deeply, his hands and ravenous mouth trailing a scorching path as he paid homage to her body.

"Anthony!" A strangled whisper escaped her, like a song to his heart. She lost her breath as the magic took over, triggering her quiet surrender.

30

Celine woke slowly and stretched. His scent still lingered on her skin and the sheets. She pulled his pillow to her cheek, inhaling the last vestiges of him, savoring her memories of their night of love taking over her thoughts.

She rolled out of bed and went to the window, pulling back the drapes. There was nothing more beautiful than a sunrise over a vineyard.

And nothing worse than waking up to it alone. She'd expected that. Anthony had gone back to his guest house before dawn after they'd made love one last time before the sun rose and Savannah awoke. Warmth flooded her as she remembered his last long, intense kiss, and how it left her not wanting him to leave.

Once Savannah was up, there was no keeping her inside the house. Celine helped her into her fluffy red coat that Santa had gotten her for Christmas—the same one she had told Teddy about.

Andrew took the little girl's hand in his and took her to the barn to let her help feed the horses.

Anthony grinned as his father smiled down at the little girl as they left. "I can't remember a time when my grizzly bear of a father has been so sweet with anyone. Except maybe

Bridget."

"It's hard to resist a little girl's charm," Celine said, watching them leave.

"I can attest to that." He sent her a wink. "Especially when she takes after her charming mother."

Which earned him a smile.

She noted his eyes skimming her jeans and red sweater that molded to her figure. They feasted their eyes on each other before he curled his arm around her waist and met her mouth in a crushing kiss. Heat exploded between them. His lips left hers and trailed along her neck, setting her skin on fire.

"Ahem." A deep voice cleared his throat at the same time as knuckles rapped on the open door.

They turned to find Rob standing there with an amused look on his face. "You didn't answer your phone. Bridget says breakfast is ready."

Somehow, Celine got her heartbeat under control. Her rising blush was another matter. "I guess we'd better go."

The smell of baking bread and fresh cinnamon rolls assaulted their senses when they stepped into the main house and went straight to the kitchen. An impressive kitchen gleaming with light streaming through the massive skylight in the ceiling. Copper pots hung from hooks over the enormous island in the center of the kitchen, surrounded by several comfortable chairs.

Andrew handed Celine a mug of coffee. "I hope you slept well."

She caught Rob's grin and took a sip, hoping to hide her blush. "I did. The guest cottage is very comfortable."

Bridget removed a pan from the professional quality oven and plated the cinnamon rolls, setting them on the table.

"There's fresh fruit and bacon on the table, and Christian will have the pancakes ready in a minute."

They all sat down and ate the hearty breakfast while enjoying the view of the grounds. A family of deer passed through, delighting Savannah.

After finishing a meal worthy of a platoon full of US Marines, Andrew took Savannah to the barn to visit the barn cats. She loved the menagerie of animals he had and she would spend the entire day in the barn if she could.

The siblings cleaned the kitchen, and before Celine could sit down and catch her breath, Anthony handed her a jacket. "Let's go for a walk."

A smile tugged at the corner of Anthony's mouth as they strolled hand in hand through the sunlit vineyard. Beyond the vines, there stood a hidden spot with a bench placed underneath a large oak tree, inviting privacy. They stopped and sat down.

"This is beautiful. I could imagine myself here in the summer with a book, hiding away from the world," Celine remarked.

"Dad is taking a trip to Florida in the spring. If you'd like, we can stay here and you can do just that."

"I'd love to if I can get the time off from work."

He watched her with a warm intensity. "Do you remember when we had coffee that first time?"

She smiled. "How could I forget?"

He cradled her jaw in his hands and looked into her beautiful eyes. "That's where it all started. Love at first sight. I fell for you the moment I saw you there. I wanted somewhere romantic when I proposed…"

"Don't you think being together in bed was pretty romantic?"

He grinned, enjoying the moment with this rare woman he'd fallen in love with. "I get a do-over. I didn't think you'd mind me telling you again how much I love you. Hopefully, this beautiful vineyard is better."

Without saying another word, Anthony reached into his jacket pocket and pulled out a small jewelry box. He got down on one knee and opened the box.

She gasped at the sparkling, emerald-cut diamond ring. Her expression was priceless.

He pulled the ring from the box and looked into the eyes of the woman who held a special place in his heart. They were full of love and anticipation of what the future would hold.

"I love you, Celine. When you walk into the room, you take my breath away." He stroked her cheek, savoring the warmth of her skin. "What we have together is special. The first time I made love to you, I thought my heart couldn't handle so much emotion. I had already fallen in love with you and my love is only growing stronger. We'll have a good life together as a family. Marry me and I'll spend the rest of my life loving you and Savannah."

She faced him, close to tears. "Yes. My answer is yes. But you already knew that."

He slipped the ring on her finger and it fit perfectly. "Now it's official."

"We need to tell Savannah before anyone else."

"I'll get her and we can tell her together. Then we can tell my family." He stood and pulled her into his arms. "There's just one more thing." He lowered his mouth and kissed her with an all-consuming, breathless, soul-stealing kiss.

Celine watched Savannah skipping as she held Anthony's hand as they made their way to where she waited for them near one of the pastures.

"Mommy, are we going riding?"

Celine gave her a hug and kissed the top of her head. "No riding. We need to talk to you about something."

Savannah cast a glance at the horses in the pasture. "Are you getting me a pony?"

Anthony grinned. "We might arrange that sometime in the future. I'm sure Dad wouldn't mind."

Savannah swung her head up to look at her mother, her mouth wide open.

"We'll talk about a pony another time. I have something important to tell you. Anthony has asked me to marry him and I wanted to tell you first."

Savannah tipped her head, clearly considering that bit of news as well as a six-year-old could. "We're getting married?"

"Yes, Mommy is going to marry Anthony and we'll be a family."

Savannah reached out for Anthony's hand. "You'll be my daddy?"

Anthony kneeled down to her level. "Your father in heaven will always be your dad. I will have the privilege of being your *bonus dad*. I will do my best to honor your father's memory and love you and be there for you as he would have. Are you okay with that?"

"Will you live with us and walk me to school?" she asked.

"It would be my pleasure to walk you to school."

Celine met Anthony's eyes, eager to hear Savannah's answer. "Sweetheart, would you like us to be a family?"

Savannah smiled broadly and wrapped her arms around Anthony. "When are we getting married? Can I be a flower girl and wear a pretty dress?"

Celine's smile grew wide at her daughter's approval. "You absolutely can be a flower girl. We wouldn't have it any other way."

Anthony threaded his fingers through Celine's, and they walked hand in hand toward the house. He couldn't hide his emotions covering his face as they stepped into the house to announce their engagement to his family.

"What's up, bro? You look a little flushed. Is all well in *Anthony-land*?" Christian teased his brother.

He smiled. "Couldn't be better."

"A beautiful woman at your side will do that." Christian winked at Celine.

She blushed.

Anthony pulled Celine closer to his side, leaned down, and kissed her. "I don't disagree. We have an announcement."

All eyes turned toward them.

He gazed at the woman he was in love with. "Celine has agreed to become my wife."

Rob and Christian gave their brother a congratulatory hug and clapped his shoulder.

Bridget went to Celine and brought her in for a deep hug. "We're going to be sisters now. I am so happy for you and Anthony. But then, I've known you'd end up together ever since you met. Never seen my brother fall so hard, so fast."

A broad smile crept across Andrew's face. He went to Celine and hugged her before doing the same with his son. "This calls for a bottle of my best champagne. Rob, will you grab a bottle of apple cider, too? I want to toast my son, future daughter-in-law, and my first granddaughter."

Tears shimmered in Celine's eyes at Andrew's instant acceptance of Savannah.

EPILOGUE

Celine's mother, Marie, helped her slip into the cool satin of her wedding dress. The ivory colored strapless dress hugged her body in all the right places.

"Let me zip you up," Linda said, as she tugged at the back of the dress, and then moved to look at her. "You look beautiful. Thank you for letting me be a part of your special day."

Celine hugged Dex's mother for a long moment, fighting powerful emotions. She couldn't help but think of her first wedding years ago to Dex. "You are family and always will be. My day is so blessed by having you here."

"I'm sure Dex is smiling down from the heavens," Linda said. "He would be happy for you."

Celine felt in her heart he would be. "I love you, Linda. Thank you for everything." Tears welled in her eyes, well aware of how much time Linda spent helping Marie with the wedding planning and the emotions it must have brought her.

"No crying. It will ruin your makeup," Bridget said.

It had been a hectic time with having the wedding in Connecticut when Celine and Anthony lived in San Francisco. Andrew had offered to host the wedding amongst the vineyards on his estate. However, traveling across the country would have been difficult for Celine's elderly grandparents, and they had the wedding in her hometown to accommodate them.

Marie and Linda took care of all the arrangements, consulting with Celine about flowers and details over Facetime. They reserved the ballroom at the historic colonial hotel nearby, and taste tested the menu Celine and Anthony had selected. The women wanted everything to be perfect and enjoyed putting the wedding together, while Andrew insisted on paying for everything.

Celine only had to find a dress—Bridget took on the duty to help her—and show up. Her head spun just thinking about the enormous undertaking her mother and Linda had taken on as wedding planners.

But you wouldn't know it by seeing the smiles on each of their faces. That Celine had found love again after losing Dex years before thrilled them. Finding love twice in a lifetime was a rare, special gift.

With misty eyes, Linda and Marie watched the emotional moment when Celine turned to face herself in the floor-length mirror.

For a moment, Celine didn't quite recognize the woman staring back. Her professionally done make-up, along with the soft curls pinned back on one side of her head and cascading down her other shoulder, and the dress—was nothing short of breathtaking.

"My daughter is a beautiful woman," Marie said with pride. "But I always knew that."

Celine took a deep breath. "I never thought I'd be so nervous."

"There's no need to be. Anthony is a wonderful man," Linda said.

"Mommy, is it time to get married?" Savannah asked with enthusiasm.

"Almost. Before we go, I have something for you." Celine reached into her purse and pulled out a small velvet pouch. Savannah watched as Celine opened the pouch to reveal a pair of diamond earrings. "Your father gave these earrings to me on our wedding day. I thought you'd like to wear them."

"They're so pretty, Mommy."

Celine helped Savannah fasten them to her ears. "You look beautiful. Daddy would be so happy to see you wearing them."

She choked back tears, watching Savannah twirl in her dress, her little cherubic face looking so much like Dex.

Celine turned toward Bridget. "And this is for you, my friend."

Inside the velvet pouch held a stunning gold necklace. "It's beautiful. Thank you," Bridget said, teary-eyed.

Celine and Savannah picked up their bouquets, and for a moment they stood side by side, smiling at their reflections in the mirror.

"Can we wear these dresses forever?" Savannah asked with a huge smile covering her face.

Celine returned her look of joy. "You may wear it whenever you like."

Celine's father knocked on the hotel door. When he stepped into the room and saw her, he wore a proud smile. "Sweetheart, you're stunning."

"Thanks, Dad."

His gaze went to his granddaughter. "Savannah, you look as beautiful as your mother."

"I'm ready to get married, too."

They all laughed.

"We should get going," he said, waving the ladies toward the door.

Celine held Savannah's hand all the way to the small chapel on the grounds where the ceremony would be. Inside, a solo acoustic guitarist strummed romantic love songs. Celine's brothers, Connor and Daniel, looking especially handsome in their military dress blue uniforms, took Marie and Linda's hands and placed them through their arms, and escorted the ladies to their seats. Savannah, looking sweet as sunshine, started down the aisle carrying her miniature bouquet. Bridget followed.

Celine's father took that moment to gaze lovingly at his daughter, emotion filling his eyes, and he kissed her cheek. "You have a good man waiting for you. I'm happy you found each other."

"Me too, Dad."

He offered her his arm. "Are you ready?"

"Yes."

Heads turned as guests watched Celine and her proud father make their way down the aisle. But her gaze was only for one man. The man who loved her. The man she would spend the rest of her life with. Her heart ached with all the love she felt for him.

Anthony stood next to his brothers, smiling proudly as he watched his bride every step of the way. When she reached him, her father kissed her on the cheek and placed her hands in Anthony's, and stepped away to join her mother.

Anthony's fingers closed over hers. He said his vows with an intensity that moved her, making her realize how deeply in love Anthony was with her. She loved this man and couldn't believe she could be this lucky twice in a lifetime.

After the ceremony, the photographer took dozens of photos of the bridal party and family. Music from the live band filtered outside, and by the time they went inside to the ballroom, the party was in full swing.

Celine introduced Anthony and his family to her friends and extended family. Wine flowed and dinner was served and enjoyed by all.

When it was time for a toast, Celine's father grabbed the microphone. "There's something my father told me when I was a young man. I've never forgotten it and never will. He said, 'Life has hardships, ups and downs along the way. But the genuine power of a man is in the smile of the woman beside him.' Never forget his words, young man, for as my wife often reminds me, *happy wife, happy life.*"

He hesitated for a moment, fighting back his emotions. "I see the smile on my daughter's face. She's happy. Never forget to tell her how much you love her. Do it every single day and you'll continue to see that beautiful smile." He raised his glass of champagne. "To my beautiful daughter, Celine."

Marie lined up all the single ladies when it was time to throw the bouquet. Celine threw it back, and it went straight into Bridget's arms.

Bridget's eyes widened. "Oh no, this is not happening to me. Girlfriend, how about a do-over?"

"Not a chance," Celine said, grinning. "You're next to the altar. Deal with it."

Christian laughed and threw his arm around his sister's shoulder. "I almost feel sorry for the guy, whoever he is."

The dancing began, and after taking his wife in his arms for the first dance, Anthony next asked Savannah to dance. She gave him a big smile as he lifted her in his arms and twirled her around the dance floor.

"Mommy and I are happy you're married," she said.

"You know how much I love you and your mommy…so very much. You have the best mother in the world. She loves you and she loves me. We are truly blessed, and we will have the best life ever."

Savannah took on a serious expression. "Can I call you *Daddy*?"

Anthony's heart squeezed tight. "Only if it's what you want. I'm also fine with you calling me Anthony."

"My daddy lives in heaven now. I think it would be okay with him."

He looked straight into her eyes. The power of this little girl's trust and acceptance of him weighed heavily on his heart. "I love you, Savannah, and will always care for you as your daddy in heaven would. It would be my honor for you to call me *Daddy*." The seriousness of the moment left tears in his eyes.

Celine moved toward them and asked, "Is everything all right?"

He pulled his wife into a group hug with their daughter. "Everything is fine. It couldn't be more right." He pressed a gentle kiss on Savannah's cheek. "I do not know what I ever did to deserve a wife like you and a daughter like Savannah."

"You loved us," Celine whispered before kissing him tenderly.

Celine hadn't forgotten about Dex, or ever stopped loving him. He would always hold a piece of her heart.

Celine and Anthony understood how fragile life could be. They had each suffered tremendous heartache in their lives. And through their grief, friendship, and love, they had learned an important life lesson.

Life is the most fragile thing in the world. And love is the most precious emotion of the heart. As minutes crumble away, you must appreciate every moment, embrace love when you are lucky enough to find it, and treasure every person who loves you. For not knowing what the future holds, you may never have another moment in life to live with love.

ALSO BY SUSAN COCHRAN

The Redemption
The Vow
Under A Falling Star
Family Honor
The Key
Edge Of Trust
Ultimate Trust
Reckless Trust
The Assistant
The Interview
Shattered
Loving Only You
Chasing After You
Hello Beautiful
Enchanted By Cupid

Made in the USA
Las Vegas, NV
20 May 2025

22445512R00105